SPIRITWALKER

The Way of the Spirit: Book 1

L.M. HELM

For mom and dad,
who first showed me The Way of the Spirit,
and for all those since who have helped me walk it.

PROLOGUE

The road cut the desert in half. The desert hardly noticed the cut, split, cracked, and calloused as its skin was by long ages of unrepentant sun and wind. The road, for its part, cut straight and narrow through the desert's rocky red flesh, making a scar of soft white sand.

A man on horseback rode alone on the straight and narrow road. Now, there was nothing about the man's appearance, other than his red skin, and his black hair, and his name if you had happened to know it, to betray his nature as an Indian. He dressed like a white man, and he did so without the gaudy embellishments which so often accompany aboriginal attempts at camouflage - feathers in caps, colored stockings, and anachronisms of that kind. No, the Indian looked, from a distance, like any drab ordinary man going from one place to another.

A handful of buzzards rose into the air from a depression in the desert's skin. "Where the corpse is, the vultures gather," the Indian said to himself. The buzzards wheeled over the depression, little black points of night in the bright blue sky. The Indian pulled his horse to a stop and watched them.

"If it is dead, why fly from it?" he wondered aloud. He turned from the wheeling buzzards and looked to his right, as if consulting with a companion, but there was no one there. He was alone. "If it is eaten, why not leave?" he asked the empty air. Then, for a long time, he stared at the place. He looked intently, like a soldier being given commands, listening to every word because his life depended on his ability to execute his orders. Finally, the commands received, he nodded and guided his horse off the straight and narrow road, and toward the buzzards.

He stopped his horse at the edge of the depression and looked down into it. A donkey stood at the bottom, mightily burdened by gear - a huge chest on one side and a spiky bundle of axes, shovels, and picks on the other. On the ground beside the donkey lay a man. The Indian did not see the man at first because he was lying in the darkness of the donkey's shadow. A rope connected the beast of burden to his collapsed master. The shadows of the buzzards rippled over them.

The man had once been fat, but the desert and hardship had drained him, leaving his small skeleton to drown in an ocean of flesh. He looked like a wrung out waterskin, one that had been pecked at by buzzards.

The Indian crouched beside the man. He was filthy. Streaks of dry red desert dirt crisscrossed his white shirt. He looked like he'd been wrestling someone with bloody hands. And he stank.

The Indian put his hand on the man's chest and felt the life still pounding in him. He went to his horse and returned with a canteen. He wetted his fingers and sprinkled the water on the man's forehead. The man turned away. The Indian gently returned the man's head and put his canteen to the cracked lips.

The water hit the man's tongue like lightning. He sat bolt upright, piggy eyes flaming, and glared at his hands. The palms and the backs were red from the desert dust. He spat the precious water into them. Then he rubbed them together furiously. "Blood," he muttered. "Gotta warsh this blood..." He wiped his wet hands on his shirt, laying muddy red streaks over the dry ones. Then he wiped his hands on his pants, buffing them fast and hard on the dusty denim. He forced the cloth of his shirt down between his fingers to dry the secret crevices. Then he inspected his hands, holding them close to his bloodshot eyes and turning them so he could see both the palms and the backs. They were clean now. Very clean.

Then the man sensed that he was not alone. He turned slowly and saw the Indian. They looked at one another for a few heartbeats. Then the man's eyes rolled back in his head and he collapsed, face first, into the ground and lay there, unmoving.

The man's collapse revealed a wound, red and crusty and high up, on his shoulder. He'd been shot in the back and some time ago by the look of it.

The Indian lifted the unconscious man onto his horse, mounted behind him, and rode out of the depression, leading the burdened donkey along behind. Soon they were on the straight and narrow road, and the buzzards departed.

SPIRITWALKER

I

Snarf's parents died before they had a chance to leave any impression on his memory. So Snarf's uncle took him in. Snarf called him Unk. Unk was a short, wiry fellow whose gambling habit caused him to miss his calling as a horse jockey, the profession for which God had designed his rail-like body. Unk never married, again because of his gambling, and treated Snarf rather less well than Snarf would have preferred to be treated, again, because of his gambling.

It was Unk who gave Snarf his name, perhaps as retribution for being called Unk, perhaps because, when his orphaned nephew arrived on his doorstep some 12 years ago, no Christian name was included. No matter. Snarf's name fit him well because Snarf snarfed; he'd pull air in through his nose and thrust his forearm across his nostrils at the same time. These combined actions made a snarfing sound. It was a sort of nervous tick he had. Remember, he was an orphan. And he was a boy, and all boys are a little bit icky, so we must not judge him too harshly.

Unk and Snarf owned and operated The Six-Gun Saloon. It was the only saloon in Amity, and they gloried in their monopoly. The Six, as Unk and Snarf affectionately called her, got her name from an ancient Allen revolver mounted behind the bar. The revolver had belonged to Unk's father and Snarf's grandfather, who, come to think of it, was the same person. Unk had called him Pap, and so the pistol was called Pap's Pistol.

Pap's Pistol had three defining characteristics. First, it was massive. It was massive because it was old. The Egyptians don't make pyramids like they used to, the Romans don't make empires like they used to, and so the Americans don't make guns like they used to. It is a fact of nature that things, even people, shrink as they age. Second, Pap's Pistol was mysteriously black, black like the hulls of the beetles that hide under tombstones on moonless nights. And third, it was loaded. Snarf spent many an afternoon watching the lead-gray slugs pupating in the big round barrels and wondering what the gun would feel like as it bucked in his hand and sent one of those burning slugs into the heart of some notorious outlaw. He often wondered how he'd spend the reward. Sometimes he wondered what it would be like to be kissed by the lady he'd rescued.

If Snarf's daydreams sound unrealistic or even violent to your ears, that is because you do not live in an age of fire like he did. You are, probably, a product of Modernity - a wretched, cold, antiseptic thing obsessed with the baleful lights produced by electrified silicon. Snarf, you must understand, lived in an age of fire: when a boy could go outside, put his back to his family's cabin - a cabin he'd help make - and see an alien world. Wolves howled at night. Indians hunted scalps with tomahawks. Outlaws marauded. Every waking moment you tingled with the knowledge that you were living in the valley of the shadow of death. There were no seatbelts. It was exciting. It was exciting because you knew you were alive.

Snarf emerged from his dark bedroom into the weird world

of the pitch-dark saloon. The candle he carried made him look like one of those deep sea fishes with the light dangling from its forehead. The chairs, turned upside down on the tables because Unk had made him mop before going to bed, cast their pointy shadows on the sparkling floor. He went up the stairs. At the top of the stairs, there was a balcony that overlooked the saloon. On the balcony, there was a door. Snarf knocked on it.

Someone on the other side grunted.

"General'll be here soon," Snarf said.

Another grunt.

Snarf went back downstairs and wound his way through the tables toward the saloon doors. His candle glittered in the glass of the lanterns that rested in the center of each table. He stopped. He looked back up at the closed door on the dim balcony above. Unk was probably going to sleep through the shipment; he usually did. Snarf snarfed. Then he put his candle on a table and carefully, oh so carefully, lifted one of the overturned chairs and set it upright on the floor. Now he could get at the lantern. Unk didn't let him use the lanterns because they were for the customers, but Unk was asleep.

Snarf carried his shining lantern through The Six and went out the batwing doors onto the porch. Sure enough, there was General's cart lumbering down the street toward him. General looked a bit like a decrepit Santa Claus. This early in the morning, his white beard was mussed and his eyes were gooey with sleep. He wore a suit of yellowed long underwear, desperately in need of darning, and a filthy night cap a yard long with a little ball at the end that once had been white and puffy like a hare's tail but looked now like the stem of a half-blown dandelion. The massive pile of goods in the back of his cart swayed as he stopped.

"Where's that crippled turtle you call an uncle?" General asked.

"Asleep."

General did not approve of Unk because, when he paid his invoices, he paid them late. Snarf and General carried in the supplies together. It was quite a load: kegs of beer, crates of liquor, barrels of salted pork, a side of smoked beef, and on and on it went, all because today was "FREE" Lunch Day at The Six.

A year ago, Unk had returned from an unsuccessful gambling jag in Ithaca, breathing words of prophecy of the fortune they would make if only they gave out free lunch one day a week. Snarf, who was the cook, was dubious. Unk, ever the gambler, painted "FREE LUNCH" on a shingle and hung it out to dry that very day.

The fiasco began innocently enough. Hungry men popped in wanting to know what the catch was. They squinted when Unk said there wasn't one. They sat, looking round for the other shoe that they were sure was about to drop. And, my, how they marveled - their expressions gave St. Thomas a run for his money! - when a free lunch, prepared by Snarf himself, was placed before them.

Word spread through Amity in a flash, and the locusts descended. Snarf and Unk ran out of everything inside 15 minutes. But Unk tried again the very next week and this time there *was* a catch. Unk amended his sign with a parenthetical, which had the added benefit of justifying the previously unnecessary quotation marks around "FREE." The amended sign read:

"FREE" LUNCH
(must buy drink)

But this was no catch at all. It was, in fact, just what the hearts of the good men of Amity yearned to do. They took to the catch like fish in water and "FREE" Lunch Day became a weekly institution, far outstripping the Sabbath in popularity and observance and serving as a financial windfall for Snarf and Unk. At least it would have, had it not been for Unk's gambling habit.

Finally General's cart was empty, The Six's larder was full, and the desert sky was white with dawn. General handed Snarf the invoice. Snarf snarfed at the total.

"I thought not," General said, shaking his head. "You tell Eugene to bring his winnings by later today or there'll be hell to pay." Then he climbed into his cart, groaning on account of his age and his gout. He took up the reins but stopped because Snarf was standing by, waiting for something.

"What?" General asked.

Snarf's eyes flicked to a rolled up paper on the cart's seat.

"Oh, yeah," General handed the paper to Snarf. "I don't know what it is you see in them things."

"The customers like em."

General snorted, "Customers got nothin to do with it."

Before Snarf could protest, General flicked the reins. Once he was gone, Snarf eagerly unrolled the paper. It was a Wanted poster. The man pictured on it was named Flint. Snarf was a little disappointed because the picture was a drawing not a photograph. He preferred the photographs because they were the real live faces of the outlaws. A drawing was just someone's best guess. But the bandana that covered the outlaw's face and the nasty scar under his left eye saved this drawing from unexciting ambiguity. The details added an air of menace and mystery to Flint, who was wanted dead or alive for $1,000, for robbery and the murder of an officer of the law.

Typically the backs of bars in Snarf's era were decorated by bottles of liquor backed by a mirror, to make the collection look more extensive than it really was. The Six had both the liquor and the mirror, in addition to Pap's Pistol, but The Six's mirror was entirely obscured by Wanted posters. They covered the mirror like autumn leaves. Some were so ancient that they'd yellowed, and their corners had curled. Others were as fresh and as brown as butcher's paper. Snarf put a dab of honey from a pot he kept under the bar on the back of Flint's poster. Honey worked just as well as glue, and it was handier. Then he climbed onto a barstool he'd retrieved and went hunting for a good spot to paste Flint. But there wasn't an empty space available. He had some posters on the wall of his bedroom, but that space was reserved for the ones he'd heard or suspected had been caught. Flint was too fresh for that, so Snarf did his best: he covered the face of some unreliable looking lady worth only $100 for the crime of "walking the street on the Lord's Day." Snarf had no idea what that meant or why it was a crime, so covering her was no great loss.

Snarf inspected his mosaic of villainy. If he caught them all, which is what he wanted to do more than anything in the world, he'd probably be a millionaire. There were murderers and cutthroats and arsonists and larcenists and confidence men and notorious women and gangs and loners and every sort of scum Satan had invented.

The palms of Snarf's hands began to itch. Pap's Pistol was within reach. Unk's door was still closed, and all was quiet. He shouldn't. He really shouldn't. He should just climb off the stool. But the lantern's light caught on the smooth shiny metal inside of the pistol's ring trigger, making it glitter like a gold wedding band. Snarf reached for it.

"What're you doin?" Unk asked.

Snarf clambered down, leaving Pap's Pistol in its place. "I was just‑ we got a new poster. I was puttin it up."

"We," Unk muttered, amused by the harmless lie. Then he glared, "Where's your candle?"

Snarf quickly relit his candle in the illicit lantern then blew the lantern out.

Unk looked haughtily down at his recalcitrant nephew,

hoping to instill a sense in Snarf of the gravity of his crime. That done, he turned to go back to bed.

Feeling suddenly impetuous, Snarf held up the unpaid invoice. "General says you better bring him your winnings." He regretted the words as soon as they left his mouth.

Unk stiffened. Like all gamblers, he believed himself a winner. Any insinuation to the contrary was an offense not to be brooked. "Mop the floor," he ordered.

"I mopped it last night."

"And then you and General made tracks in it with your little dirty feet, so you will mop it again." Unk slammed his door.

Snarf looked up at Flint's Wanted poster. Only the outlaw's eyes were visible in the shadows cast by the dancing candle flame. Snarf made a gun with his fingers and shot Flint dead.

2

The vast horde of men crammed shoulder to shoulder at the bar, knee to knee around the poker tables, and eye to eye over the billiards expected their food fast and their drinks instantly. Snarf worked like a dervish.

Many of the men declared Snarf made a better steak than their wives. They didn't tell their wives that, obviously, just each other. And indeed, Snarf did make a great steak, but then he made great everything because he had an uncanny knack for the one vital element in cooking: heat. Mastery of herbs and spices and the balance of fat and acid eluded him, but he had a knack for heat, for fire, in spades, as Unk would say. He knew when his stove was hot enough and when it had gotten too cool, and he knew just how much wood to add to bring it up to where it needed to be. When a steak went on, he started no timer and consulted no clock but flipped it at precisely the right time and took it off at precisely the right time, every time. Snarf might not have known much by today's standards, but he knew fire, because he was a product of his age.

Each plate got a steak, a scoop of potatoes, a scoop of beans, and a thick slice of cornbread. There was too much salt in the beans and potatoes - that was Unk's trick, to encourage drinking. Between serving the plates and flipping the steaks, Snarf made the lucrative drinks. Thankfully the simple men ordered simple drinks, but Snarf could make anything. He'd been tending bar since he was six. He'd been delivering drinks since he could walk.

With a tray on his shoulder, he threaded his way through the tables. He peeked at Unk's cards as he passed: black aces and black eights, the Dead Man's Hand. Now, despite its name, the Dead Man's Hand is actually a good hand, and, knowing this, Unk had bet heavily on it. Unfortunately, it was not good enough. Unk slapped his cards down, and another man raked in his chips. Unk was bust. Consequently, so was Snarf.

Snarf handed the plates and drinks to their purchasers. He stuffed the money, which was hardly enough to make a dent in General's invoice, into his apron. But Unk grabbed his arm as he passed and plunged his hand into the pocketed money.

"At least let me get it to the register," Snarf protested.

"Gotta strike while the iron's hot," Unk said, slapping the money down and reaching for more cards.

Cashless and annoyed, Snarf went back behind the bar and made a single plate, but this one was different: hold the beans and double the cornbread. He grabbed the honeypot from its secret place under the bar and carried the food to a man sitting alone at the far end of the bar where he could look out on the entire saloon. All the man's outfit, from his hat to his boots, was black, except for the silver on his pistol, spurs, and the badge which stood out on his broad chest like the North Star. His name was DC and he was the sheriff of Amity, and he was Snarf's hero.

Snarf slammed down his food.

"Hey, easy. I don't like my potatoes mashed."

"Someday," Snarf declared, "one of them outlaws is gonna walk in here."

"Walk in here? Yeah, and what'll you do?" DC asked as he poured a copious quantity of honey over his cornbread.

"I'll yank Pap's Pistol down and blast him."

"Blast him? Yer awful young. You think you got the stomach for killin?"

"Sure I do. He'll be worth ten thousand dollars, at least. I'll be able to get outta here. Then Unk can make his own free lunch and mop his own floor for all I care."

"Where you gonna go?"

"I'm gonna go after the rest of em and not quit till I get em all or I'm a millionaire. I'll be a bounty hunter, like you were. The best ever."

DC shook his head as he chewed his honeyed cornbread. "You don't wanna be a bounty hunter."

"Why not?"

"It's cold at night."

"I don't care about that. I'd be tough. 'He's one tough barve,' that's what they'd say about me."

"Who's gonna say that?"

"All of em!" Snarf stabbed his finger at the Wanted posters.

"All of em! I thought you killed em?"

Snarf glared at the sheriff, who cracked a smile, "I'm sorry. I'm bein contrary."

Snarf snatched the sheriff's second piece of cornbread - for revenge.

"Tough barve?" DC protested. "Yer a mean barve."

Snarf took a teasing bite of the cornbread, but the sheriff was no longer amused. His eyes had slid past Snarf. They were on the door. "Don't look now, deputy, but this might be your chance."

Purl stood in the doorway of The Six.

Purl was Amity's Goliath, and he was a purebred Philistine if ever there was one. Legends innumerable of his strength and cruelty blanketed the country. Most notable among them was the tale of the time he'd thumped an elk on the top of its head with his bare fist, on the hard bony place between the antlers, and kilt it dead. Or so the story went. The elk had been within arm's reach, the story went, because it had sneaked up on him while he was sleeping to investigate his person for eatables. Purl ate the elk itself raw in a single sitting, the story went.

A hush fell over The Six. All eyes were on Purl.

Purl lifted his little round hat - it wasn't little, really, but they don't make hats in his size - and mopped his acre of brow. He replaced his hat and made his way toward the bar. Every head swiveled to follow the giant.

Snarf considered leaping up and snatching Pap's Pistol. It was close enough...

DC, without taking his eyes off Purl, shook his head. His hand had moved stealthily to hover over his pistol. The wooden handle was varnished black. It shone like obsidian and was as cool as the hand hovering over it.

Snarf's hands were hot and sweaty. He wanted to wipe them on his apron, but he was too scared to move.

Purl towered over Kit, a farmer sitting at the bar, and glared down at him. Kit evacuated his stool - his barstool, you understand. Then Purl put one massive boot on the stool and hoisted himself up. The top of his hat flattened against the ceiling.

More than a few heads turned sideways at the sight of such a big man on such a small stool.

Then Purl began rifling his pockets.

All eyes went to DC. They saw his hand near his gun, and they saw there wasn't a drop of sweat on him or a bit of tension in his body. He was as loose and as ready as a whip.

Purl produced a piece of paper. It had been folded many times, in a childlike way, to keep its message secret. His big fingers worked the folds apart. He had trouble with the final fold, so he licked his thumb and found the reinforcing moisture helped his cause. Then, to the disbelief of many, and the great enhancement of his legend, Purl began to read.

"I have seen the light," his voice was as big as he was, though his reading had a hitch in its giddy-up. "Last Sundee, I were born-again. I were warshed by the blood of Jesus Christ. And cleaned of all my sin." He caught his theological error and corrected it: "Sins."

A smile played at the corner of DC's lips. He took his hand off his gun, put his elbow on the bar, and put his cheek on his fist. This was gonna be good.

"Since that time, wicked spirits have not touched my tongue ner I have lain with my woman-"

"She survived the maiden voyage?" one wit whispered to his friend, who coughed into his beer.

Purl went on undeterred, "-with who I-" but he got tangled. He brought the paper right up to his face, almost touching his nose, "with *whom* I had been living in gray vase" (he meant grievous) "sin. I have re-pen-ted. And so should yew." Purl cleared his throat and glanced at his pupils who, he was surprised to see, were attending to him studiously. "Yew can repent by voting in support of the National Prohibition Party and it's candy-date, James-"

The Six erupted. A whole steer's worth of steak flew at Purl from every direction. Kit avenged and covered himself in ever-lasting glory by kicking the stool out from under Purl. The giant's fall smote the floor, rattling the teeth of those nearby, who fell on him with blows.

DC broke through the press, hauled Purl up, and, with assistance from Unk and encouragement from all, threw Purl out.

Purl rolled to a stop at the black-booted feet of the entire Ladies League, a small flock of pious women who stood arrayed like wolves outside The Six.

"How dare you!" Easter, the head of the pack, bellowed.

She advanced on them all, with one arm raised like the Statue of Liberty. "How dare you assault and waylay this man! This pillar of our community!" The pillar of the community lay on the ground being daubed with hankies. "You!" She stabbed her black-gloved finger at Unk, "You, sir, and your foul establishment are a menace. A smudge," she rubbed her finger over her cheek to illustrate what a smudge he was, "on the face of our righteous community." Something caught her eye. "Sheriff!" she shrieked, pointing again at Unk, "Arrest him. Arrest him for corrupting a child."

All eyes went now to Snarf, who was standing next to Unk.

"No child - so innocent and pure! - should be made to distribute wicked spirits!"

"I like wicked spirits!" Snarf shot back. The men roared their approval, patted him on the back, mussed his hair, and punched his shoulders.

Poor Easter's heart nearly gave out. Sputtering, she turned to her flock, who had gotten the pillar of the community back on his feet. "Do not look back, ladies; remember Lot's wife." She spread her arms like a mother hen, bidding the ladies turn and retreat. They obeyed, with eyes downcast and averted.

Purl, however, looked back. A week of abstinence is a hard thing for any man to bear, and Purl, with his prodigious appetites, feared he lacked the strength to carry on.

"No, Purl. You have been bought with great price. Remember: you are a New Creation."

Purl stopped, which meant the ladies had to stop too. They tugged and pulled at him, whispering, "Come, Purl," and "You can do it, Purl, dear," and other such encouragements.

Purl lifted his giant arm and pointed, not at the men on the porch of The Six, but at something in the road beside them. "An Indian," he announced.

3

DC drew in the time it took the next fastest man to get his hand on his pistol. The sheriff held his gun at his hip, aimed up at the Indian, ready to blow him off his horse. As the others drew, DC observed that the Indian had no gun of his own - no weapon even, just a small knife sheathed at his side. But the white man, lying across the Indian's horse like a hunting trophy, told tale enough.

"State your business," DC demanded.

"We found this man in the desert. He needs care."

"'We,'" DC asked as the men looked at one another nervously.

Snarf wished he had Pap's Pistol, so he could point it at the heathen savage like everyone else.

"The Son of the Great Father and myself."

"Son of the Great–" DC waved away the rest of his own question. "Nevermind. Get down."

The Indian dismounted and stood before the sheriff just as calmly as if he'd been invited to share a drink.

DC reached out slowly, so the Indian would have time to look down all the barrels pointed his way and contemplate the consequences of any sudden movements, and took the knife from the sheath at the Indian's belt.

The Indian didn't seem to care.

DC gave the knife to Snarf. He held it reverently. The deer's antler that formed the handle made the knife feel alive in a way that his kitchen knives never had. Snarf would've bet Unk anything that this knife had tasted blood. Heck, it had probably taken a scalp or two!

DC stepped up to the Indian and searched him for hidden weapons.

Snarf brandished his knife at the Indian, in case he should try anything with DC so close. His movement gained the Indian's attention and he looked at him. Face-to-face for the first time, Snarf realized that the knife he was threatening the Indian with had, just seconds before, belonged to the Indian himself, and he'd allowed it to be taken without a fight. Shame washed over Snarf. He lowered the knife.

"What's your name?" DC asked as he searched the Indian.

"Redskin."

"That some kinda joke?"

"No."

"Where's your gun?"

"I do not have one."

"Don't have one. Stupid for anyone to travel without a weapon."

"I am not alone."

"Yeah, you mentioned that. What's the matter with him?" DC prodded the unconscious white man.

"He needs water and food and a doctor. He has been shot in the back."

"Did you shoot him?" Kit demanded, brandishing his gun like Snarf had the knife.

"I do not have a gun."

Kit blushed, lowered his pistol, and muttered some feeble excuse for forgetting the obvious.

DC wasn't buying the Indian's goodie-goodie act. "Where's your partner?"

"Partner?"

"The son of the great padre or whoever."

The Indian pointed to his right. DC and the others saw only empty air, so they followed the direction of the finger out into the desert.

When you see Indians, be careful. When you do not see them, be twice as careful, was a proverb they all knew by heart.

DC took a deep breath. "All right," he said, taking the Indian by the arm. "You're comin with me. You," he looked at the men of The Six, "ride out and search for this chief's son or whoever. I'll join you after I lock him up." DC started to lead Redskin away, but Redskin didn't move.

"What are you going to do for him?" he asked about the unconscious white man.

"He can stay here," Snarf volunteered. "At The Six, I mean."

"No," Unk protested. "We don't take boarders."

"C'mon, Unk-"

"I said no. We don't have the room and-"

"He can stay in my room."

"That's-"

"He can stay in my room for as long as he needs to," Snarf announced, looking to DC for support.

"I own the saloon!" Unk cried. "I own your room! *I* decide who stays in it, not you!"

DC pointed at two men. "Carry him into Snarf's room." The men moved to obey.

"Sheriff, I must protest-"

"Then protest, but he's stayin here. I don't have anywhere else to put him."

Unk caved.

"You tell me the minute he wakes up," DC ordered Snarf. "You hear me?"

"Yes, sheriff," Snarf beamed, and he ran after the two men who were lugging the unconscious man inside. He scampered around them, ran between the billiard tables, and opened the door to his bedroom. They dumped the man on his unmade bed. It creaked under the load.

One of the men waved his hand and made a face, "He stinks."

"Don't forget his stuff," Snarf reminded them.

"I ain't no porter. Sheriff said to bring him in here, and that's what I done."

"You gotta take orders from the deputy!"

The men just laughed as they walked away.

"You are *not* a deputy," Unk glowered from the doorway.

"I almost am."

Unk towered over Snarf. "I am permitting this... thing to stay here because the sheriff insisted, but I hold *you* personally responsible for any pecuniary damages *I* incur. Do I make myself clear."

Snarf glared at Unk and snarfed defiantly. "I gotta bring in his stuff."

The donkey stood outside, nearly capsized beneath the tremendous weight of all the gear. There were burlap sacks of beans and onions, all manner of foodstuffs, clusters of picks and shovels tied together like grapes and, on the other side, serving as a sort of ballast, there was the chest. The great big monstrous chest. Snarf could have been buried in it if he were dead and had room to rattle about in the afterlife.

He worked at the knot that tied it all together, but it was too tight from all the weight straining against it. Then he remembered the Indian's knife. He drew it out of his apron pouch and cut the rope. All the gear crashed to the ground, and the donkey sighed - actually sighed - with relief.

Snarf hauled in the burlap sacks first. Then returned for the digging tools. He had to drag the chest. Halfway there he stopped, afraid he was gonna bust a gut, and noticed that the corners of the chest had etched four little trails in The Six's wooden floor. He hoped Unk wouldn't notice.

He shoved the chest into the corner beside the bed. For a moment, he stood there panting and wondering what was inside. The chest's lock was prodigious, so the secrets it held must be enormous. Then he got a whiff of the man's stench and decided it wasn't worth the risk. He settled for grabbing as many of the Wanted posters that he'd pasted to his bedroom wall as he could reach.

With a handful of posters, Snarf left his - now the man's - bedroom and wished almost immediately that he had not. Unk was on his hands and knees, inspecting the newly etched trails in his saloon's precious floor. He rose and came at Snarf with fury in his eyes. "You're going to clean this place up. And then you're going to clean it again and again and again until you've made up for your carelessness. And then you're going to repair those scratches. And then you're going to clean it all again! Do I make myself clear?"

The Six was trashed from the episode with Purl - food everywhere, tables and chairs overturned, and pools of liquor all over the floor.

Snarf nodded like a condemned man.

"Good." Unk turned to leave, then saw the wad of posters in Snarf's hand. He snatched them away before marching upstairs to his bedroom.

"Those aren't even the best ones!" Snarf shot.

Unk slammed his door.

Snarf picked up the mop.

4

When Snarf finally finished cleaning, the tips of his fingers hurt from scrubbing, and his back ached from sweeping. Not a soul had come into The Six nor passed by the big windows that looked out on Main Street in all the time he'd been toiling. No, Amity was battened down tight, her citizens living in fear and trembling of the Indian, or Indians, whichever it was, prowling about the place.

Snarf leaned lazily on the bar and teased a bead of water across its smooth surface, and wondered if he'd survive if life continued to pass by at its present rate. Then the door to his former bedroom burst open. The man, who'd been unconscious just hours ago, stood swaying in the doorway like a tree in a gale.

"Whisky!" he bellowed.

Snarf, startled and surprised, stared at him.

The man stabbed a finger at him, "You!" he bellowed, marching toward the bar. "Whisky! Now!" When he said "now," he pointed his finger down at the bar in front of him. "Are ya deaf?! Whisky!"

Snarf snatched a bottle and poured a shot. It was down the man's throat in a flash.

"Another."

Snarf poured.

Up went the man's clean hand with the glass, and down went the whisky. "Another."

Snarf poured.

The man drank.

Unk scurried down the stairs.

"Another."

Snarf poured a fourth shot, and the man drank it just as fast as he had the first. When he put the glass down, Snarf filled it, but Unk interrupted the pattern by offering his hand. "Eugene Brides."

"Billy," the man said, and they shook. "I'm a miner by trade. You do much custom?"

"Pardon?" Unk asked.

"I asked if you do much custom out here."

"Not as much as I'd like."

"Yeah, well, sorrows come in battalions. Any womens for hire?"

Unk was offended. "Absolutely not."

"Good. Hirable womens draws crowds." Billy downed the fifth shot of whisky, which had waited patiently for him. As he set it down, a thought occurred to him.

"Hey!" he exclaimed. "Where in creation am I?"

"Amity," Snarf said.

"Amity?! Never heard of it." Billy held out his glass, which Snarf began to fill.

"It's just south of Ith-"

"Nope!" Billy cried. "Don't tell me where it is. Don't relate it to nothin. As the Good Book says, if I'm lost, I cain't hardly be found." He drank his sixth shot, put the exhausted glass upside down on the bar so Snarf couldn't fill it again, and rummaged in his pockets.

"D'you need a doctor?" Snarf asked with unfortunate timing.

"Doctor? Do I look like I need a doctor?" Billy glared.

"Redskin, the Indian, said you'd been shot in the back."

"Indian?" he asked, still searching his pockets while he glared at Snarf. "Somebody steal your rudder, boy?"

Evidently the alcohol had sanitized the man's memory, and Snarf didn't like being called crazy, so he shut his mouth.

Billy turned to Unk, "Yer boy nuts? You got madness in the family?"

"He's not my son."

"Chariots of fire!" Billy swore as he gave his pockets a thrashing. "Ah," he said, finally finding what he was after. He thumped a gold nugget the size of a chicken's egg onto the bar. "I'm a simple man. I want just five things: bacon, eggs, whisky, soap, and water." He ticked them off on his fingers as he listed them. "You keep em coming and you won't even know I'm here. Tell me when that runs out," he meant the nugget, which Unk and Snarf had not ceased to stare at since its miraculous appearance, "and I'll git you more. Hey..." he growled, his eyes darkening as they took in all the Wanted posters. "You got some kinda head-hunter on the premises?"

"Oh, no," Unk answered, afraid his new golden goose was about to fly the coop. "Those are Snarf's. He collects them."

"You collect em?!"

"For fun," Snarf explained, his voice cracking. He snarfed.

Billy looked at Unk for an explanation.

"He thinks, one day, one of them might come in here. He'll shoot him and get rich. It's silly."

But Billy didn't think it was silly. "You watch fer all them fellers?"

Snarf nodded, not trusting his voice with speech.

"You got all them faces in yer brainpan?"

Snarf nodded again.

Billy lunged across the bar and seized Snarf by the collar. Snarf went stiff as a corpse, hoping that if he didn't fight back, Billy would release him. But Billy didn't. Instead, he hauled Snarf down the bar toward his bedroom.

Unk scrambled out of their way.

Snarf's frozen feet dragged across the polished floor. Billy threw him into his room, then turned to Unk, "We'll only be a minute." He slammed the door shut.

Snarf trembled in the corner by the chest.

"Si' down," Billy ordered.

Snarf sat on the chest.

"On the bed, ya idjit."

Snarf quickly relocated to the bed.

Billy took an old, weathered rosary from around his neck. The rosary had a key on it that was quite a bit larger than its companion, a weathered crucifix. Billy unlocked his big chest with the key. As he fished inside, he explained, "I require yer assistance, boy."

"Me?"

"Shut-up an listen. I need you to keep a weather eye open for one Matthew Craney." Billy took a paper from the chest and thrust it into Snarf's hands. It was a photograph of two lines of men in military uniforms standing outside a fort. There was an American flag. The sign on the fort read Fort Bowie. Billy pointed a jagged fingernail at the face of the commander, who had his hand on a cannon. "He on one of yer famous posters?"

Snarf shook his head.

"Didn't think so. You got his visage in yer mind's eye?"

Snarf nodded.

"Keep it there," Billy snatched the photograph from him,

"and come runnin' to me if he shows his ugly mug. Come-prend-ay?"

Snarf nodded again.

"Now git," Billy said. Snarf went for the door—

"Wait!" Billy cried. He tossed Snarf a bit of gold the size of a pea. "That's to keep yer memory up to snuff. Matthew Craney's his name. You see him, you come to me."

Snarf nodded and escaped. Billy shut the door behind him with a bang.

Snarf stood there with his back to the door and the little gold nugget clutched tight in his fist.

"You all right?" Unk asked.

Snarf couldn't believe it. The Army, the Army of these United States, was hunting the man now occupying his bedroom! That meant... that meant Billy was an outlaw! Didn't it? And Billy'd paid him, so now he was an outlaw too! Snarf snarfed.

"Snarf?"

"I gotta... I gotta go tell DC," he said, walking on rubber legs toward the door.

"Tell him what?" Unk asked.

Snarf didn't answer. He broke into a run, hitting The Six's doors at a dead sprint. They clapped behind him.

"Snarf?!" Unk called after him, but Snarf was long gone.

5

Snarf soared down Amity's empty street, buoyed as he was by the news he carried. He crashed into the door of the little building marked "Sheriff," and it burst open.

Redskin sat up on his cot in the jail cell.

Panting in the doorway, Snarf looked around. DC often complained that the jail was really a jail inside a jail, and Snarf was inclined to agree with him. The tiny building imprisoned a kitchenette, table, and desk. DC's bed was in an alcove tight enough to make a submariner sweat. A wall of iron bars cut the little space in half, so the prisoner had just about as much room as the sheriff.

"Where's DC?" Snarf asked.

"He is out with the others," Redskin said, "searching for my companion."

"He say when he's gonna be back?"

"He did not."

Snarf looked at the desk. Papers and pencils littered its surface. He could write a note, but he feared his letters weren't up to snuff.

"Is there a message you'd like me to give him when he returns?"

The Indian's clairvoyance broke through the last of Snarf's defenses. "Tell him Billy's wanted by the military! Some commander named Matthew Craney's after him and wants him real bad!"

Redskin absorbed the news slowly. "Billy is the man I found in the desert?"

Snarf nodded.

"And Matthew Craney is after him?"

Snarf nodded again.

Redskin looked to his right, as if there was someone there with him in the cell. Snarf craned his neck, but Redskin was definitely alone. The Indian turned back to Snarf. "Is Matthew Craney coming here?"

"I dunno. Billy's sure scared he'll come. Just give DC the message." Snarf turned for the door.

"Wait," Redskin said. He was holding a bit of leather out between the bars. It was the sheath for the knife now rattling around in Snarf's apron pouch, the knife that had belonged to Redskin until DC took it from him.

Snarf approached the bars cautiously. The Indian didn't move a muscle. Slowly, Snarf reached out. The leather sheath was cool and soft. He slid the knife into it. "Thanks," he said.

"Be careful," the Indian replied. "Death is very near."

Snarf held up his sheathed knife. "I'm ready."

"You are a Fleshwalker. You are not ready."

Snarf had no idea what a Fleshwalker was, and he didn't really care. "Just give DC the message."

"We will," Redskin said.

The "we" brought Snarf up short again. There really wasn't anyone else in the cell. Was there?

. . .

31

On the porch, Snarf looked back at the closed door to the jail. That Indian sure wasn't like any Indian he'd ever heard of. No weapons - it was like meeting a man without skin. Still, he had the sense that the Indian didn't need weapons. He felt dangerous and peaceful at the same time. Snarf had never met anyone like him.

He moved his apron aside, loosened his belt, and slipped the sheath onto it. The knife felt good on his hip. He stuffed his hands into his pockets and hopped off the porch in that way reserved only for boys without a care in the world. When he landed, he felt something bounce in the apron pouch. It was the gold nugget Billy had given him. Snarf adjusted his course away from The Six and toward a building on the other side of the street. "General's General Store" its sign proclaimed in green letters.

"Where'd you git it?" General asked skeptically, peering at Snarf's bit of gold, which he held between his ancient finger and thumb.

"I earned it," Snarf said.

General's bushy eyebrows went up, "Quite the tip."

"How much?"

"Eh, it's a little pea of a thing. And it's lonely too," seeing the nugget as a reflection of his own status as a widower of some 30 years, General sounded genuinely grieved. He recovered himself, "Now if you'd told me you struck it rich, I'd give you more. On credit."

"How much?"

"Mmm..." any assessment of value pained General.

Snarf interrupted, "General, have you ever heard of Matthew Craney?"

"Name seems vaguely familiar. Why?"

"He's in the army. I thought-"

"I was not and am not a General!" General exclaimed. "Sufferin Christianity! What I wouldn't give to go back and stuff my daddy's throat at my christenin!"

"Then," Snarf asked sheepishly, "why does everyone call you General?"

"Cause it's my name! Dad-blast it all! Isn't that why everyone calls you Snarf? A dollar and a quarter," he announced, his assessment of the gold complete and a bit below fair market value on account of his aggravation.

It was more than enough, though. Snarf pointed at a gunbelt and holster hanging on the wall behind General. "I want it in black."

"Don't come in black. Newd, if you'll pardon the expression, is all."

"Can you order a black one?" Snarf asked hopefully.

"Fer another dollar."

Snarf didn't have another dollar.

"Out here, shippin' and handlin's pretty dear, sonny."

He also didn't have time to wait. Craney could come at any moment, and he needed to be ready. Snarf saw the solution, "I'll take the belt and that shoe polish."

"Hey, yer a clever one!" General said as he set the things on the counter. No sooner had they touched down than Snarf snatched them up and bolted for the door. "Wait! Don'tcha wanna receipt?"

"No," Snarf called over his shoulder.

"Be sure you let the polish set!" General shouted after him, "And tell Eugene he owes me!" but the tinkling of the bell above the door obscured General's final order.

6

How easily excitement blinds us to oncoming danger! In Snarf's case, the poor boy walked right into it. Head down, fastening on his new gunbelt as he walked into The Six, he failed to notice Unk lurking behind the bar.

"Where'd you go in such a hurry?"

Snarf's head snapped up. His position was entirely compromised; while crossing the street from General's, he'd put the tin of shoe polish in his mouth so his hands would be free to put on his new gunbelt. He blinked stupidly. Then released the gunbelt. It sagged around his knees. He took the tin of shoe polish out of his mouth. "I tried to find DC," he said.

"Why?"

"Cause I had somethin to tell him."

"Which was?"

Snarf glanced at Billy, who was passed out at the bar with his arms wrapped around a mountain of poker chips. Atop the mountain, like a cherry on a Sunday, glittered the gold nugget. Their biggest windfall in ages, and Unk had already gambled it away.

"He's out cold," Unk reassured him.

34

"He's wanted by the army."

"How do you know?"

"He told me. Showed me a photograph and everything. Some commander named Matthew Craney's lookin for him."

"And you didn't tell me?"

"I just did."

"Is there a reward?"

Snarf shrugged, "He paid me to keep watch for Craney and let him know if he shows up."

"And so you purchased an oversized gunbelt and a tin of shoe polish?" Unk shook his head.

"Better than losing it all in a game of blackjack."

Unk's eyes flashed. "Come get me when supper's ready, deputy." He went upstairs into his bedroom, leaving Snarf alone with the unconscious Billy.

Snarf stepped out of the sagging gunbelt and carried it to the bar. He pried open the shoe polish, found a rag, and set to work. Eventually he made supper by reheating a couple left-over Free Lunches and carried one up to Unk. Billy slept through everything.

Dusk came. Snarf looked out the window for DC and the hunting party, but there was no sign of them, so he went back to his belt and the polish. Sometime after nightfall, the job was done. The gunbelt was black as sin. He put it on.

It was a man-sized belt, that's why he'd had such trouble with it earlier, so he had to tie it in front. If you've ever done this, you'll know that belts don't tie very well. An uncomfortable ball of leather hung just below his belly button. And the holster felt wrong, too. It was so light, it flapped when he walked, sort of like a broken wing.

Snarf looked up at Pap's Pistol. Getting it down was usually no problem - he'd done it before - but this time, Billy was in the way.

He snarfed.

He climbed up onto the bar, carefully put one foot on either side of Billy, and leaned... He hooked Pap's Pistol by its ring trigger with just one finger. He slipped the huge gun into his holster and pushed himself upright again. He carefully stepped over Billy and climbed down off the bar.

Now the holster felt great, thick and heavy on his thigh. The resistance of it when he walked made him feel strong.

Ten paces from Billy, he stopped, feet shoulder width apart, hand poised over Pap's Pistol, muscles tense... "Hey," he said, making his voice extra low and gravelly. "There's only two ways outta my town: on yer feet or inna box."

Billy didn't move.

Snarf drew, but the pistol got hung up on the holster. He wiggled it free eventually and pointed it at Billy's back.

Well, he thought, he'd have time to learn how to draw. In the meantime, he needed to keep tabs on his first wanted man. He leaned against the billiard table and inspected Pap's Pistol. It wasn't a revolver, that had always been obvious; it was a saw-handled pepperbox pistol, heavy as a brick and a sight more deadly.

See, revolvers have only a single barrel, fed by a revolving chamber, but pepperbox pistols have multiple barrels, anywhere from 6, like Pap's, to a crazy 24. The barrels, however many there are, are welded together in a mass, making the gun unusually front-heavy. They rotate as the gun's fired, like a Gatling gun. Looking down the barrel of a pepperbox was like looking into a beehive, an experience not many wanted to repeat.

"Snarf?" DC said, standing in the door with his hands resting on the tops of the batwing doors, his hips cocked, and his eyes clear and assessing. "Everything ok?"

"I was- he- you gotta arrest him, right now! And send a message to the Army that I got him! Do you think the reward's gonna be a big one?"

DC smirked at the boy's enthusiasm, "A big reward, huh?" and lit a cigarette.

The sheriff's apathy burst Snarf's bubble. "Didn't Redskin give you my message?"

DC nodded and blew out the smoke. "He did."

"And you're not gonna arrest him?"

"Nope."

"Why not?"

"Cause Matthew Craney ain't in the Army."

"He's commander of Fort Bowie," Snarf insisted, "Billy showed me a photograph."

"*Ain't*. I said he *ain't* in the Army."

"What d'you mean?"

"Matthew Craney *was* commander of Fort Bowie, back when you were about half the size you are now. Washington told him to take out an Indian chief, Strong Bull that was burnin and rapin folks all over the territory. Craney got his scent, tracked him, cornered him and his warriors in a cave. He tried to smoke him out," DC took a drag of his cigarette.

"What happened?"

"Smoke filled the cave. There was a lotta screamin and hollerin, but not a single Indian came out. Later, Craney sent his men in. All they found were a bunch of dead women and children-Indians, but still."

Snarf shivered.

"It got in the papers. Washington wasn't happy. Someone busted Craney down. Way down."

"So he quit the Army?"

"Quit the army? He deserted. Took a few soldiers with him. They turned outlaw and have done pretty well. Turns out a little discipline goes a long way in that profession."

"What about Strong Bull?"

"Vanished. So, you might say, in the end, Washington got what it was after. Same can't be said for Craney."

It took Snarf a moment to absorb - he'd taken an innocent man into custody. Not an auspicious way to begin his career as a deputy. He holstered Pap's Pistol. "What are we gonna do?" he asked.

"We need to know how he comes into it," DC nodded toward Billy. "What d'you know about him?"

"His name's Billy. That's all."

"That's all. He had a lot of stuff on that donkey. You get a look at any of it?"

"Just a bunch of picks and shovels and stuff. Some onions and beans. I think he's a miner."

"What about the crate? That chest? You get a look in it?"

Snarf shook his head, "But he got the photograph out of it. It's locked with a big key that he wears round his neck."

"He wearin it now?"

"I dunno. I guess so."

"Well, go have a look."

Snarf blinked. Was DC really suggesting *he* look for the key? The key Billy wore around his neck?

DC patted his revolver. "Don't worry, deputy, I'll cover you."

Snarf swallowed the lump in his throat. "He- he's a angry drunk. He's crazy."

DC made a face. "Crazy? How bad can he be?"

"Bad enough, I bet."

DC slid down the bar and examined Billy up close. He picked up the empty whisky bottle and sloshed the dregs around. He tsked to himself. "Any man who gets drunk on whisky's doin it wrong," he said. Then he drew his pistol and used its barrel to lift the matted hair that covered Billy's neck. Sure enough, there were the rosary beads. DC slipped them off Billy's neck. "Alright," DC said, holstering his gun, "you cover me. I'm gonna see what I can see." He headed for Billy's room.

Snarf tried to draw Pap's Pistol, but it got hung up again.

He tugged and pulled frantically on it, but it wouldn't come out of the holster! DC had his hand on the doorknob when Billy sat up.

"You gotta warrant?" Billy asked.

Calmly, with his hand still on the knob, DC turned. Billy sat at the bar with his gun drawn, and Snarf stood behind him, still trying to get Pap's Pistol out of its holster.

DC saw that he was defeated, so he smiled at Billy, "Sure don't." He took his hand off the doorknob and leaned casually against the wall, tucking his thumbs into his gunbelt.

Billy plucked his gold nugget off the top of the poker chip pile and swaggered up to DC. "You get pokey again," his pistol tickled DC's ribs, "and I'll fill you up. Come-prend-ay?"

DC put his hands up in mock surrender, "I wouldn't mess with a tough old barve like you."

Billy sneered, went into his room, and shut the door. DC grinned at Snarf, who was crushed by his failure. "Don't worry about it, deputy. Guns and holsters have to get to know one another a while before they slide in and out easy. Next time, you'll come through," he patted Snarf's shoulder as he walked out of the saloon.

Snarf watched the sheriff's black silhouette ripple across the big windows as he walked home to the jail. Snarf tried again, and this time, Pap's Pistol came out easy, its six barrels leveled at the sheriff's shadow. Frustrated and ashamed by the weapon's treachery, Snarf shoved it back into the holster.

7

The sound of sloshing water woke Snarf. He knew right away that it was coming from his (now Billy's) room, but he lay still, hoping it would stop.

It didn't. And Billy started mumbling drunkenly.

Snarf sat up on the billiard table. Since he'd given away his room, the billiard table was the only place he could think to sleep. *Did he cut himself?* he wondered. A faint glow of candle-light oozed from beneath Billy's door.

"Here's a spot!" Billy hissed, sloshing the water in his basin. "Who'da thought men'd so much blood in em?!"

Snarf crept to Billy's door, head cocked and straining to hear what was happening. It sounded like Billy was washing his hands.

"Hands'll never be clean again," Billy mumbled. Now Snarf was close enough to hear the soap squelching between the man's fingers. He *was* washing his hands. What for?

Snarf had blown it with DC earlier. He wasn't going to blow it now, not with such a ripe chance. He put a hand on Pap's Pistol to keep it from making a sound, lay down on the floor, and peered through the gap under the door. He could see very little; only the bed, with its dismembered sheets hanging onto the floor, and Billy's bare white feet, laced with ghostly green veins.

Billy made a noisy, wet, nasally sound, not unlike one of Snarf's snarfs. "The smell of blood still," he muttered. Then he plunged his hands back into the basin, splashing soapy water onto his broken yellow toe nails. He sobbed, "Ain't there enough rain in sweet heaven to warsh em clean?"

Then the sloshing stopped.

"No," Billy moaned. "No there ain't, cause I still got it. I still got all that I done the murder for."

Murder! The word shot through Snarf like lightning.

"But, if I were to get shod of it..."

Billy's toes turned and pointed right at Snarf!

His heart pounded against the floor. He couldn't move! He wanted to. Every part of him wanted to jump up, run straight through one of the big windows, and sprint through town, screaming for DC - but he couldn't! He could barely breathe.

Billy's toes, putrid and rank, stopped just inside the door, inches from Snarf's face. His heart hammered the floor. Surely Billy's bare feet could feel it pounding!

Billy opened the door and looked down at Snarf, who was laying prostrate, like a pilgrim before the Pope. Snarf peeped up at him. "Boy," Billy said, "I'm not long fer this world, an I got things I need to get clear of fore I go." He turned, walked heavily, like a sick man, to the bed, and sat.

Snarf didn't understand, but he found he could move again, and Billy hadn't murdered him. So, quite relieved, he got his rubbery legs under himself.

Billy took the rosary from around his neck and looked at the crucifix for a long time. "There's a divinity that shapes our ends," he muttered, "rough-hew em as we will." He tore his eyes away from the rosary and looked at Snarf. His eyes were as empty as a moonless night.

"Craney trusted me," Billy confessed, his voice husky from all the whisky he'd poured down his throat. His fingers felt the contours of the cross and the tiny crucified Christ frozen on it, but his eyes were sightless, lost in memory. "He trusted me so much, he-he put me in charge of the loot. The gold. There was so much gold... Craney knew if he gave it out all at once, every man'd leave, set himself up as king somewheres, and live high and mighty. Craney couldn't have that. So he tells me to hide the gold and we'll dole it out slow and steady. A kinda dividend. Me and some others that he trusted, we found a hidden place. Some Indian place right there on the mountain. That's where we hid it. We hid it real good. But seeing that much gold all together like that, it- it's powerful hard on a man. It took me."

"What took you?" Snarf asked.

"The gold. Gold can grab a man sure as the devil. Fills him up with a sort of hordin emptiness that he'd do- well, he'd do anything to fill, but the only thing the emptiness wants is gold. But there ain't enough. Not in El Dorado. Not in all the world. Some calls it the Ecstasy of Gold. Me, I calls it lust. And death."

The little hilltops of Billy's hunched spine rose and fell as he breathed. There was a hole in the back of Billy's shirt. The flesh there was red and puckered, furious at the lead rotting under it.

"Who shot you?" Snarf asked.

"There were six of em stackin it high, making a wall out of it - a wall of gold, if you can imagine such a thing - and there I were watchin it rise. My hand went to me gun and I thought, 'Six men, six shots; and I'm the only one who knows where it's hid; mighty providential.'" Billy turned to Snarf, "And it were providential. Mostly."

Billy looked down at the crucifix, and he seemed to see it for what it was for the first time. He hissed through his teeth, like a man does when he's being burned, and let it fall. The key made a heavy singing thump on the wooden floor before the string of beads strangled it to silence. The crucifix lay on top, upside down.

Billy flexed his hands. The palms were milk white, the cleanest hands Snarf'd ever seen. "I made a kind of a map," Billy said. "It's in me chest." His earnest eyes begged Snarf, "Will you- will you take it from me, take it off me shoulders as it were. I don't think I'll make it-" he started to glance up toward heaven but thought better of it, "I don't think I'll make it with such a load on me back."

"Sure," Snarf said.

Billy put his arm around Snarf and squeezed him. The stench was unbearable. "You'll need me key." He pointed at the key lying under the crucifix at their feet.

Snarf bent to pick it up, but Billy seized his arm and shook him hard. "Don't you let him have it! Don't you let Craney lay a finger on it!"

The shadow Snarf had thought he'd seen reaching out for him had possessed Billy. Rage contorted the miner's face, his eyes burned with black fire, and his foul breath hissed between his yellow teeth.

"I won't," Snarf whispered, terrified. "I promise I won't let Craney have your gold."

The shadow released Billy and his hand fell limply from Snarf's arm and lay on the bed like a dead thing. "Ain't mine no more. It's yourn." Billy lifted up his eyes again, this time without faltering, "D'you see this, oh Gawd? Ain't mine no more." His drunken eyes searched the ceiling for some sign that he'd been heard. But none came. "Come, come, come, come, what's done can't be undone." Billy lay down, putting his back to Snarf, the rosary, the chest, and, it seemed, to the whole world.

Snarf picked the rosary up; Billy did not intervene this time. The crucifix was light, wood probably. The key was iron, hard and heavy. Snarf went to the chest. The key went in easy. It turned a little rough, though, grinding on the dust of all Billy's travels. He lifted the heavy lid. There was no gold in the chest that he could see, just an old duster jacket. He took it out. Still no gold. And no sign of a map either. Just the photo. Craney didn't look so mean. Also, there were some weathered folios, plays by Shakespeare. Snarf set them aside. Still no sign of a map - wait. There was a cylindrical leather case tucked in the back corner of the chest.

The case had a seam running around it with a snap on one side and a hinge on the other, and it had a loop of string, a sort of shoulder strap, dangling from it. Snarf popped the snap and the case opened like a clamshell. A piece of leather was rolled up inside. He took it out.

It was a drawing of a snarling coyote. It had been burned into the leather, stroke by stroke, with a hot nail or something. It was a hard, cruel drawing, made all the harder and all the crueler by the crude instrument that'd carved it. Slather covered the coyote's teeth, and his eyes flamed in the candle-light, as if they remembered the heat of the nail that had drawn them and hated that it had lacked the power to give them sight. The coyote also seemed to have a wound in its forehead. There were lines there which gave the impression of gushing blood. The blood ran down between the coyote's eyes. The stream separated around the muzzle then re-coagulated under the jaw and poured all the way down to the bottom of the piece of leather, like a waterfall.

"Find the coyote," Billy said, "and you'll find the gold."

The coyote? Snarf wondered, but before he could ask, Billy was snoring. Snarf rolled the drawing up, stuffed it back into

44

the case, and put the strap over his shoulder. Then he threw everything back into the chest and locked it.

He turned for the door but stopped. He looked at the rosary in his hand. He had no need for it, but maybe Billy did. Snarf put it on the chest. Then he left quickly, eager to get to DC as fast as his feet could carry him.

8

But there was a beautiful lady behind the bar. She was trying to read the labels on the moonlit liquor bottles. The moonlight embossed her silhouette with silver, and Snarf's heart jumped. If Unk had been awake, he'd have had a coronary. Snarf had never seen the woman before in his life, but her name was Jewel and every inch of her was worthy of the name.

"I wonder," she said, turning to him, "if I might have some gin?"

"Sure," Snarf answered, relieved his voice hadn't cracked. He fetched the appropriate bottle while she made her way back around to the customer's side of the bar. She walked with a cane, a simple black thing with an ivory grip that clicked on the floor as she walked, but she did not need it. Snarf was certain that if she'd had a book on her head like he'd seen pictures of ladies doing, it wouldn't have wobbled an inch. A cat could have slept through a thunderstorm on that book.

Snarf poured the gin. Jewel rested her hands on the bar. She wore gloves - the kind of gloves made out of netting - and the peach flesh of her hands showed through the netting. Snarf stared at the little bits of flesh like a fool.

And completely forgot he was pouring a glass of gin. "Ah!" he cried, but it was too late. Gin poured over the sides of the glass. Sheepishly, he wiped the bar and slid the too-full glass to her.

"Thank you," she said. The sparkle in her eyes told him that she meant it. She raised the glass to her red lips, so steady was her hand that she didn't spill a drop. She took such a dainty sip that, when she put the glass down, Snarf couldn't tell if she'd even been able to taste it.

"That's fine," she said. "Now, I am looking for my brother, and I have it on good authority that he's staying here. William is his name. He is in difficulties and requires my assistance."

"There's no William here. Just me and my Unk," Snarf said.

"Your... Unk?"

"Uncle, ma'am, beg pardon. He owns this saloon."

Jewel smiled. Snarf gripped the bar to keep from fainting. "Just you and your Uncle?" she asked. "How quaint. But, I do wonder, who were you speaking with a moment ago?"

"In there?!" Snarf pointed to Billy's room. Jewel nodded and the moonlight caught in her doe eyes. "Oh!" Snarf exclaimed, and he laughed like an idiot for no reason he could think of. "That's just Billy. Don't mind him."

"Billy, you say? Did you know that Billy is often a nickname for William?"

Snarf shook his head, feeling for the first time a tendril of fear slithering up his spine. There had been something cold in the sparkle of Jewel's eyes as she asked the question.

Her smile widened, "Well, now you do." She turned to the empty bar - Snarf caught a whiff of her perfume and thought he had died and gone to heaven. "Flint," Jewel announced to the darkness, "would you please let William - Billy - know we are here?"

A man, unseen in the dark recesses of The Six, struck a match, illuminating his hideous face. A red scar began under his left eye and traced its way down his cheek. The scar exploded across his mouth. And his only tooth, a long yellow canine, glinted through a great tear in his lip.

The tendril of fear that had slithered up Snarf's spine a moment ago coiled itself between his shoulder blades. This was Flint- *The Flint* worth $1,000 for robbery and murder! Snarf cursed himself inwardly for ever wanting to know what his face looked like.

As Flint lit the lantern on the table, Snarf's tendril of fear wrapped itself around his throat because Flint wasn't alone. There were five other men rising to their feet. Each of them wore what was left of a military uniform. They were deserters - Craney's men!

Flint pulled a red bandana from his pocket and tied it over his nose and mouth. Then he led the men to Billy's door and opened it, spilling candlelight into the saloon. "Wake up, Bill," he said.

Snarf could not see Billy, but he heard a sort of strangled shout, the kind a person makes when waking from a nightmare. Then the bed creaked violently. Flint's pistol came out if its holster in a flash. It boomed. Something big and heavy fell to the floor. Then, all was silent.

Jewel smiled a smile at Snarf that seemed to say, *Isn't this nice?*

But it wasn't nice. It wasn't nice at all. Snarf wished he were still asleep on the billiard table. Or, better, had been caught up in whatever tragedy it was that had made an orphan of him.

Flint went into Billy's room. Snarf heard the key in the chest, then he heard the lid go up, and the things come out. All the fear he'd felt that night paled in comparison to the lead weight of dread settling in his guts then. These were Craney's people all right. And they were here for the map. The map he had strung over his shoulder!

Unk's bedroom door burst open. He looked like an

avenging angel in his white nightshirt - an avenging angel with a shotgun. He leveled both barrels at Jewel.

She looked coolly up at him. Unk, red faced and sweaty at the thought of killing, saw he was aiming at a woman. Ashamed, he lowered his weapon. "I thought I heard a shot," he said.

"You did," Jewel replied. And somehow there was a derringer in her hand. Where it came from or how it got there, Snarf never knew to the end of his days, but it was there. And it was digging into his ribs. "And, unless you want to hear another, I suggest you put your gun down."

"If you hurt one hair on my boy's head, I'll-"

"Please," Jewel insisted, "lower your scattergun."

Snarf and Unk locked eyes. Yes, they'd had a mountain of disagreements and they'd inconvenienced one another terribly over the years, but hearing his uncle say "my boy" when it really mattered and watching him lower his shotgun to save his life, Snarf saw - really saw - the man for the first time. And he saw that Unk had given him everything.

Flint's pistol boomed again. Unk vanished in a bloody red mist. His shotgun fell and broke itself on the table beneath the second floor landing.

"Thank you, Flint," Jewel said once everything was quiet again.

Flint nodded and announced, "It's not there."

Jewel sighed and turned to Snarf, who was staring up at the empty doorway to Unk's room, but he wasn't really looking at the doorway. He wasn't looking at anything in the world. He was looking inside himself. Something was happening there, deep down. A feeling had started when Flint had shot Unk. It was a feeling he'd never felt before. His insides felt like water just before it boils and makes the kettle scream. Sort of all bouncy and on the edge of something. He didn't know what.

"I am sorry you had to see that," Jewel said. "And I under-

49

stand if you want us to leave, but we cannot leave without the map."

Finally they'd come to it.

"Billy gave it to *you*, didn't he," she said. "Just before we came in."

Snarf took the case containing the map off his shoulder and gave it to Jewel. There was nothing else he could do. She opened it. Flint came over with the lantern and they stared at the drawing of the coyote. All the sparkle went out of Jewel's eyes. "This is not a map," she said coldly. "What is it?"

"A coyote," Snarf answered, his bouncy insides making him feel impetuous.

Jewel's snakelike eyes demanded an explanation.

"'Find the coyote, find the gold.' That's all Billy said," Snarf explained.

"That *all* he said?" Flint demanded.

Snarf met the outlaw's eyes, which were really glinting now that they were there incarnate and not just ink on a poster, and decided he didn't like Flint one bit. "He made me promise not to let Craney have it," he said spitefully.

"Shame for a boy yer age to make promises he can't keep," Flint said.

"Your bandana's got a stain on it," Snarf observed cruelly. And there was a wet place on the side of the outlaw's bandana. It was where Flint's lip had been cut. The lip didn't seal up properly there, so spittle had a tendency to run down his chin when he spoke.

Flint seized Snarf and put the barrel of his pistol to his chest.

Jewel laughed, a musical sound, and put a restraining hand on Flint's arm. "My, my, my," she shook her head in disbelief, her eyes sparkling again. "Matthew's going to pull your tooth when he finds out you shot Billy without learning where he hid the gold."

"He came at me! What was I supposed to do?" Flint demanded as he released Snarf.

"You could have tried eating another bullet," she said, putting the coyote back in the case. Then she went for the door. Flint, still protesting, followed. "Oh!" said Jewel, "I almost forgot." She removed a silver dollar from her purse and placed it on the table by the door. "I'm sure this and the gold Flint left in Billy's pockets will more than account for any inconvenience we've caused."

Snarf's insides exploded. He screamed and yanked Pap's Pistol from his holster, pointed it at Flint, and pulled the trigger. Pap's Pistol did not boom like Flint's revolver. It thundered, a deep rolling sound that stretched on into infinity. A colossal noise, prophetic of the angel's trumpet blast on Doom's Day. It thundered so because every round in it went off at the same time.

Six bullets streaked every which way. One struck one of the men in the gut, and he screamed. Four buried themselves, smoking like demons, in the wooden walls and floor of the saloon. The last bullet struck the lantern by Jewel's patronizing silver dollar. The lantern shattered then exploded, splashing flaming oil all over the door and the man closest to it.

The six simultaneous shots, the burning man, the flaming door, and the man who'd taken a gutshot and was collapsing into his companions sowed anarchy among the villains. One tried to haul the gutshot man back onto his feet, but he was bound and determined to stay doubled up, to keep his insides inside. Another fought to keep the burning man away from himself. Coldhearted Flint shot the burning man down to keep him from lighting the whole gang on fire. Jewel tried to get back on her feet - the gutshot man had knocked her down - and one of the men, trying to earn points with Craney and save his own skin at the same time, picked her up like a sack of potatoes, tossed her over his shoulder, and ran toward the flaming door.

The case fell from Jewel's hand as the man lifted her. She scraped at it and shrieked at Flint, who went for it.

Snarf grabbed up a bottle of Billy's beloved whisky and tossed it at the empty space between Flint and the case. The bottle shattered. Flames erupted. Flint staggered back.

The gutshot man and the man who was helping him crashed ungracefully through one of the big windows and crawled like babies for their horses.

Only Flint and one other outlaw remained in the bar. The outlaw took a potshot at Snarf, missed wildly because he wasn't really trying, and dashed out of the saloon.

Now it was just Flint, Snarf, and the case. Flint was gathering his courage to dash through the flames and grab it when bullets tore into the wood beside him. DC! DC was outside, shooting in at Flint.

Flint swore and ran out of The Six. The others were there with his horse. He mounted, and they all rode off.

Snarf looked out from behind the bar. He was alone with the fire and corpses. He ran upstairs to Unk, put one of his feet under each arm and hove like an ox. DC met him and helped carry Unk down the stairs and toward the only unbroken window. Snarf's eyes fell on the case. Without thinking, he dropped Unk's feet and went for it.

"Snarf!" DC shouted as he shattered the window with his pistol butt.

The flames around the case leapt for the fresh air. Snarf didn't care. He snatched up the case, put the strap over his shoulder, and ran to DC. They hoisted Unk's body out of the broken window and dragged him away from the burning saloon.

9

As Snarf and DC got clear of The Six, the good people of Amity descended on them. Most wanted to help. The selfish and fearful - how often those sins go together - demanded to know what had happened.

"We heard shots!" insisted Easter, clutching her black shawl.

"Indians?" Kit asked, gun out, raring and ready to go.

"No Indians," DC announced. "Outlaws."

"We gonna go after em?"

DC shook his head. The outlaws had a head start; any pursuit would turn into an ambush in the night.

"But it's your duty," Easter insisted.

"My duty," DC mused as he looked at Snarf who was staring at Unk's body, oblivious to all around him. "General," DC called. General stepped forward. "Here's a chance to earn your name. Form a brigade. Do what you can about the fire; make sure it don't spread."

"Yes, sir," General replied, snapping a salute. He turned to the townspeople and began barking orders, which they followed.

"C'mon deputy," DC said softly to Snarf. "Let's get outta here." DC picked Unk up - his rail-thin body weighed next to nothing - and led Snarf toward the jail.

Easter and the Ladies League, along with Purl, who was not permitted to help put out the fire presently ravaging the 'devil's watering hole', watched the sheriff lead the young man away.

Redskin climbed to his feet when they came in. He'd been kneeling by his cot. He watched DC put Unk's body on his bed and cover him with the sheets. Snarf sat limply in a kitchen chair and stared at the floor.

The boy'd been through it, but there was a good deal more to get through in DC's estimation. He wasn't wrong. "I need you to tell me what happened," DC said. "If you need a minute, you go ahead and take it, but-"

"No," Snarf said, "it's alright." He took a deep breath then told DC all about Billy's confession, Matthew Craney's gold, and Jewel's untimely arrival. It was a relief to put the whole confusing mess in a row.

Snarf handed DC the case. He didn't want it or anything to do with it. "You can have it." He walked over to DC's bed and looked down at Unk's body. He just wanted everything to go back to the way it was before Billy came.

DC felt the ash on the outside of the case. He couldn't believe the kid had had the guts to snatch it out of the fire. "You're one tough barve," he marveled. Snarf snarfed. DC opened the case and looked at the drawing of the coyote.

Redskin watched from his cell.

"Billy said, if you find the coyote, you'll find the gold," Snarf explained. "Do you know what it means?"

"Means? No," DC said, distracted and transfixed by the

54

awful drawing. It was mesmerizing in a horrible kind of way, a real work of madness.

He tore his eyes from it and found Snarf looking down at his dead uncle. "Snarf," he said softly, "Snarf, listen to me. When a man gets hurt like you been hurt, he's only got two options: he can roll over and take it, or he can grab his hurt and shove it down the throat of the one who gave it to him.

"You and me," DC went on, "We'll find this coyote, we'll take Craney's gold, we'll make him hurt, Snarf. He'll hurt. I promise you, before we're done with Craney, he'll howl."

Snarf hung his head. "No," he said, "I'm not like you. I can't even draw. I think I'll just stay here. Fix up The Six..." he trailed off.

DC understood. The kid was all done. He looked again at the coyote. It did have a certain allure. And there was all that gold to think of...

General came in, wringing his singed night cap. He had bad news and didn't know how to begin. "I'm sorry, sonny. Alcohol burns awful good. We- we couldn't save her. Best we can do is hope she don't burn down the town."

Snarf looked at Unk's body. His nose looked like a snow-capped mountain under the white sheet.

DC nodded at General, and he left quietly.

After the door shut, all was silent. It isn't often that a person gets reduced to just the clothes on their back in less than an hour. And, for the second time in just 12 years of life, Snarf found himself orphaned.

DC couldn't stand to see the kid looking so pitiful. He stood up, breaking the motionless silence. "Take that thing off," he ordered, pointing at Snarf's knotted gunbelt.

Snarf obeyed and gave the gunbelt to DC. DC laughed. Snarf looked down at himself and saw that his waistline and the thigh of his pants were stained from the black shoe polish that he'd failed to let set. "General didn't have a black one," he explained.

"And why'd you need a black one so bad?"

"No reason," Snarf said.

But Redskin saw that DC's gunbelt was black.

"No reason. Well, first thing's first, you don't need this," DC stripped the holster off the gunbelt. "That pepper-box has a clip on it."

Snarf inspected Pap's Pistol. Sure enough. There was a belt clip running along the barrels. Snarf suspected that's what had gotten hung up in the holster when he'd tried to draw.

DC cut the excess leather off Snarf's belt then bored a hole in it so it could be buckled. Snarf put on his newly tailored belt. It fit perfectly. He clipped Pap's Pistol to it.

"Pepper-boxes are cheerful guns made for places without elbow room, like a poker table. You find yourself in a fracas, don't try and draw fast, cause you won't be able to. Wearing it clipped on like this, you'll need two hands to work it off your belt. So if you need it quick, just grab it, twist, and shoot from the hip. Don't worry about aim. As you mighta noticed, these things have a mind of their own."

Snarf tried DC's quickdraw method. It worked! DC put up his hands in mock surrender. Snarf couldn't help but crack a smile. DC stood beside him and turned him so they were both facing the Indian. "How do we look?"

"Like father and son," Redskin said.

Snarf felt his heart warm. Sure, he was an orphan again, but maybe this was the chance he'd been waiting for, the chance to go after outlaws and make a fortune. Maybe he could be more than just DC's deputy. "Can I see the coyote?" he asked.

"Sure." DC gave him the drawing.

Snarf looked at it. It meant nothing at all to him. But maybe... he left DC's side and went to Redskin.

"Careful," DC said, "anybody knows what or where that coyote is could get the gold."

Snarf was willing to risk it. "Billy said it was some kind of Indian thing," he explained, holding up the coyote so Redskin could see it. "Do you know what this means – where this coyote is?"

Redskin took in the drawing for a moment then admitted, "I do."

"Will you take us?"

Redskin looked to his right.

Snarf turned to DC. The sheriff shrugged; he didn't know what or who the Indian thought he saw anymore than Snarf did.

"We will take you to the coyote," Redskin announced.

Snarf grinned at DC, "Let's make Craney howl!"

But DC was studying the Indian. "Why?" he asked.

The Indian did not answer.

DC let the question hang.

"The Way of the Flesh," Redskin finally explained, "the way you are both walking, leads to death, as you have seen tonight. We will accompany you in the hope our presence may persuade you to choose the Way of the Spirit."

"We?" DC asked. "You keep sayin 'we.'"

"The Son of the Great Father and myself."

DC searched the empty cell to Redskin's right. He didn't know what the Indian was playing at, but he decided he didn't really care. Craney had hurt the kid; now justice needed to be done and the gold needed to be found. "Fine," he said, and he unlocked the cell.

"My things?" Redskin asked.

DC pointed to a bundle in the corner. Redskin hurried to it and searched to ensure that everything was there. He unwrapped a big rectangular bundle – Snarf caught a flash of gold from whatever it was – and he wrapped it up again.

DC lifted a corner of his mattress, grabbed a wad of cash he kept there, and stuffed it into his boot.

Snarf, feeling he should grab something, took a cast iron skillet from DC's kitchen. DC hadn't seasoned it properly, but that could be mended. Then he saw Unk's body, and the grim events of the night came back to him in a flood.

DC was going for the door. "Horses are in the-" he stopped.

"Who'll bury him?" Snarf asked, standing over Unk's body.

"I'll send a letter."

"Then, I guess I ought to say somethin."

DC took his hat off.

"I dunno what to say."

"I reckon you just thank him for all he did for you," DC answered. "Tell him you'll miss him and that you'll see him again in the by and by."

"Thanks, Unk, for sticking up for me there at the end. That was mighty nice of you. I'm gonna go with DC and get the man who killed you and Craney too. I don't know what'll happen after that, but I- I guess I'll miss you. I'll see you again in the by and by." His eulogy was unsteady because he was on uncertain ground.

"Grant, Great Father," Redskin broke in, "to all who are bereaved, Your Spirit of faith and courage, that they may have strength to meet the days to come with steadfastness and patience; not sorrowing as those without hope, but in thankful remembrance of your great goodness and in the joyful expectation of forever life with those they love."

Snarf, without noticing, had closed his eyes during the Indian's words. He opened them and, despite the wild night, he felt peace settling over him.

DC opened the door.

Snarf snarfed and then went out the door into the dark night, leaving Unk behind.

Amity's air was thick with smoke from The Six, and the bright fire cast harsh dancing shadows onto the little path that led from the back of the jail to the stable. Snarf could see the silhouettes of the townspeople as they fought the fire consuming the only home he'd ever known. The glowing fire and the night's smothering darkness made the townspeople look like pagan revelers around a heathen bonfire. The fact that they all had their backs to him made Snarf feel like he and the others were on some clandestine mission.

Once inside the stable, Redskin hurried to his horse. He'd been well cared for by DC, and the Indian thanked him. DC threw his saddle over Boss, his big black stallion, and ordered Snarf to get Billy's donkey.

Snarf went to the stall and fumbled the bridle over the donkey's head amateurishly. Thankfully, the donkey knew what he was about and gave the inexperienced boy some aid. Snarf led him out of the stall in time to see DC lift a massive bedroll onto the back of Boss's saddle.

"You'll ride with him," DC pointed at Redskin.

Most young men in the West learned to ride practically as

soon as they could walk. Not Snarf. He'd learned to sweep at three, how to cook a hash at four, and by five he'd been able to read the labels on the whisky bottles. But riding was almost completely outside his experience. The idea of riding behind an Indian filled him with dread.

Redskin put out his red hand. Snarf wondered if it would be red-hot to the touch, but there was no other way onto the horse. Quickly, he grabbed Redskin's hand. It felt like every white hand he'd ever shook. Then he was in the saddle. In the saddle with an Indian. What a night!

DC led them out of the stable.

Before they reached the straight and narrow road that ran through the center of Amity and into the desert, they found their way barred by the entire Ladies League, including poor Purl. After getting the brush-off from DC outside the flaming Six, Easter had decided that an ambush was necessary to recapture the initiative. She commanded her troops back to barracks with orders to dress for battle - the surprise of the shooting and the fire had left them poorly arrayed in night dresses and other such immodest civilian garb. That done, they'd regrouped and staked out their position. DC, Redskin, and Snarf had walked right into the trap.

"What can I do for you ladies?" DC asked with all the politeness he could muster.

"Where are you taking that boy?" Easter asked. It was universally understood that "that boy" was Snarf.

"I dunno," DC answered.

"You don't know?" Easter asked, smelling a half-truth.

"Sure don't. But this here Indian - Redskin, he calls himself - he says he can lead us to the place the outlaws come from. We mean to ride there and bring justice. After all, it's my duty."

"And you intend to take the boy with you as a member of your... posse?" she asked dubiously.

"Sure do."

"I am sorry, sheriff, but we cannot permit such an unlawful action."

"Unlawful?"

"Not unlawful legally, you understand, but unlawful morally."

"Say, I don't understand."

"Well, it's like this: We have it on good authority - we saw the body - that the boy's custodian, Eugene Bridges, has put down his mortal coil."

"He's dead, yeah, and in need of a Christian burial after we're gone. Is that something you ladies would enjoy?"

Easter beamed, "We'd enjoy it very much." Then she realized she'd been distracted. Her face darkened. "It is only right that you remand custody of the child to us," she demanded.

"Remand custody?"

The ladies nodded.

"To you?"

"Yes," Easter said. "Surely, even you must see that we are far better equipped to introduce the boy to righteous living than are you yourself."

"Me myself?"

"Yes. We can have the effects of wicked spirits corrected inside a fortnight, can't we, Purl?"

There was a slight delay as Purl's lagging mind came to the realization that he was to speak. "Yes, ma'am," he said.

"Tell him, tell the sheriff, Purl, what you told me last Lord's Day."

But Purl couldn't remember.

"About your mother..." Easter reminded him.

"Oh! Right. Sheriff, I confessed that I wished I'd been raised by these here ladies instead of my own heathen mother, God rest her soul. They'd have saved me much tribe-you-lation."

"See," Easter said triumphantly. "What do you think of that?"

"Nothin," DC said.

The Ladies League exploded with expostulations. "How could you?!" and "To be so dismissive of the Lord's work!" and many other such sayings cannoned out of them. Easter herself, however, was silent as a general while her soldiers launched their fusillade. She observed the effect the barrage was having on the enemy - namely, none - and took decisive action. She put up a hand, and her ladies fell instantly silent. They were well disciplined.

"Ladies, we must remember Paul's letter to the Romans; we are to be subject to the high powers. DC is our sheriff. He is the law," Easter bowed her head. The other ladies did likewise. Purl, once he caught on, took off his hat.

DC smirked. He'd never been bowed to before.

"Sheriff, may we lay our hands on the boy and bless him?" Easter asked.

DC looked at Snarf. Snarf shook his head. He had no desire to be blessed by these hags.

"Sure," DC said, feeling magnanimous.

The ladies and Purl surrounded Redskin's horse and laid their hands on Snarf, who was feeling rather uncomfortable to be so pawed at.

"Oh Lord," Easter intoned, "be merciful to this child on his many adventures. Keep him from danger. Keep him from sin, but above all, keep him out of the clutches of those who would destroy his soul!" Her hand clamped on Snarf's gunbelt, and she pulled with all her might. The other ladies took the signal from their leader and they pulled too. Snarf cried out and clung to Redskin. The horse danced nervously under them.

"DC!" Snarf cried.

"What do you want me to do? Shoot em?!" DC hollered as

he grabbed at the reins of their horse to keep the ladies from being trampled.

Snarf was coming out of the saddle and losing his grip on Redskin when salvation came from the most unexpected person - Purl.

Purl used his massive hands to bat away the clutching ladies. "Go!" he shouted as Snarf got himself back in the saddle.

"Purl!" Easter shrieked.

"Ride!" Purl bellowed.

Redskin gave his horse a kick, and they shot away.

"Atta boy, Purl!" DC hollered back at the big man who now found himself being mobbed by the women who moments ago believed themselves his spiritual bulwark.

Snarf clung to Redskin for dear life as the horse throbbed beneath him. What little experience he'd had on horseback had been limited to walking. He squeezed his eyes shut and wished he could do the same with his ears - the wind was howling.

Soon, however, the throbbing horse and screaming wind became ordinary. Snarf opened his eyes. The moonlit desert stretched as far as he could see. The saguaro looked like little crosses, marking the graves of those who'd fallen without water. The gently rolling hills, painted blue by the moonlight, looked like the bottom of the ocean. And the stars, which shine much brighter in the desert than they do anywhere else, speckled the black sky like sunshine on oil.

They rode up one of the hills and stopped. Amity would have looked like a child's block town if not for the burning Six. The impossibly long shadows of those fighting to keep the fire away from the neighboring buildings made the town look like it was under assault by giants.

"Let's go," DC announced, turning Boss into the darkness.

But Redskin waited just a moment, letting Snarf have one

last look at the town that had been his home for as long as he could remember. Unlike his parents, Amity had made an impression on him. "Are you ready?" Redskin asked.

"Yeah," Snarf said, "I'm ready."

Redskin turned his horse away, the darkness swallowed them, and Snarf did not look back.

11

Snarf woke slowly. Every part of him ached, and his legs throbbed with each beat of his heart. They'd ridden for what seemed like an eternity last night, and when they did finally stop, Snarf had been asleep before DC made the fire. Redskin had covered him with a wool blanket, and that was the last he knew.

Now it was golden morning and cold, shockingly cold in the desert. He stretched his legs under his blanket - he'd curled up in the night to keep warm - and his knees and ankles popped. He groaned.

DC did not hear the pops or the groan. DC couldn't hear anything over the sound of his own snoring. He was snug as a bug inside the gloriously warm and padded bedroll that experience had taught him to bring.

Redskin was gone.

Snarf sat up. The Indian's blanket lay, neatly folded, by the fire, but the Indian himself was nowhere to be seen. His horse, however, hadn't gone anywhere. He was asleep between Boss and the donkey.

Snarf tossed his blanket aside and was immediately embarrassed to see the black stains left on his pants by the shoe polish. He put his gunbelt on, to cover the stains, and headed into the desert.

Once he got away from DC's snoring, Snarf felt the desert silence descend on him. Deserts, be they hot or cold, are the quietest places. No animals skitter through the undergrowth because there are no animals and there is no undergrowth. No wind whistles through the leaves because there is no wind and there are no leaves. There is not even the drip... drip... drip... of water onto rock because there is no water. No, deserts are quiet, like bones.

So it will come as no surprise that Snarf heard Redskin before he saw him. He followed the voice and found Redskin sitting on the ground in front of a rock. The rock was about the height of a chair's seat. Redskin was looking up at it, as if he was looking up at someone sitting on the rock. Also, the Indian had a book open across his lap. It was very large and gilded with gold. Sometimes he would read from the book and sometimes he would look up at the empty place above the rock. And sometimes, and these were the times that unnerved Snarf most, the Indian would look at the empty air above the rock and say nothing. He would just sit there with the silence of the desert pressing down on him and his eyes locked on nothing.

But it was peaceful, almost too peaceful. Snarf felt as if some sound or noise had suddenly gone missing and left behind only a void. It made him uncomfortable, and he had no desire to disturb the Indian, so he crept back to camp.

He got the fire going, heated the skillet, and fried some of the bacon he'd found in DC's saddle bags. He also found a pot and some coffee. The smell of the coffee woke DC. He shivered, "Cold," he muttered, pulling his bedroll tight around himself. "Where's Redskin?"

"Over there," Snarf pointed.

"Talkin to hisself?"

Snarf nodded.

"That Indian's crazy," DC said as he poured himself a cup of coffee and blinked the sleeping sand out of his eyes. "It's too early to talk to anyone, much less yourself."

"You think he's dangerous?"

"Dangerous? I never met an Indian yet that wasn't. Now no more jawin til I got my coffee in me." He went silent. He sat hunched like a turtle in his bedroll and sipped his coffee. Snarf prodded the cooking bacon.

Redskin returned just as the bacon finished. "Good morning," he said.

"Morning," Snarf replied.

DC grunted.

Redskin tied his pack, which contained the big book he'd been reading from, to his horse, then joined them at the fire.

Snarf was halfway through cutting the bacon into portions when he realized the knife he was using belonged to the Indian. "You want it back?" he asked, hoping in his heart of hearts the Indian would let him keep it.

"I have no need for it," Redskin said, taking his bacon. "Perhaps you will find it useful."

Snarf beamed. "You scalp anyone with it?"

"No."

"Well, that's ok. I still sure do appreciate it."

Redskin took a drink of the coffee. His eyes widened.

"Somethin wrong?"

"It's good!"

DC laughed. "Snarf, he's the best cook in Amity. Learned everything he knows the hard way, too. Idn't that right?"

"Sure is."

"Trail may be long, but at least we'll eat good," DC proclaimed.

"How long are we gonna be out here?" Snarf asked.

"A few weeks," Redskin answered.

That was not the answer Snarf and DC had expected. "A few weeks!" Snarf exclaimed. "But there's hardly enough food for today!"

"He's right," DC said.

"We will go to Ithaca. It is on the way, and it is sufficiently large to supply our expedition."

"Ithaca," DC said, thinking it over. "We'll hit Ithaca today. Where is this coyote that's so many weeks away?"

"Colorado Territory."

"Colorado!"

"It is just over the border. Do you have enough money for supplies?" he looked at DC's boot, where he'd stuffed the wad of cash.

"Yeah, I got enough."

"Once we get the gold, I'll pay you back from my share," Snarf offered.

"That raises an interesting point," DC said, livening up a little. He downed the rest of his coffee. "How we gonna divvy up the loot? I'm fundin the expedition, so obviously I get paid back whatever I put in. Then we each get a share, but you," he looked at Redskin, "you're our guide. What's your fee?"

"I will charge no fee, and I want no share," Redskin said.

Two surprises in one morning was two too many in DC's estimation. But he could tell that the Indian wouldn't budge.

"I think he should get something," Snarf said. "A few weeks is a long time."

"I agree. Sides, makes me nervous to have a man aboard gratis. How much?"

Snarf shrugged, "A hundred dollars."

"Sounds like a lot, but if Craney has half as much gold as I think he does, a hundred dollars won't amount to a fly's fart. That's settled then - you get a hundred dollars whether you want it or not. So, it's to Ithaca for supplies, then Colorado Territory for the gold."

"What about Craney?" Snarf asked. "How're we gonna deal with him?"

"How are we gonna deal with Craney? Only a handful of guys deserted with him, and you softened a bunch of em up last night. And besides, these gangs of desperados never hang together long. No honor among thieves and all that. Plus, now that his gold's missin, I betcha Craney's up to his teats in mutiny. And we got surprise on our side; that counts for just about everything. We'll probably find this coyote alone and abandoned and eager for friendship. You," he turned again to Redskin, "we're gonna have to get you a gun."

"I will not carry a gun."

That was the morning's third shock, and it was the greatest of them all. "Why not?" DC finally managed to ask.

"Because I will not awaken my flesh."

"Awaken my flesh," DC muttered. He didn't have a clue what the Indian was talking about. Nobody did, probably. He turned to Snarf. "Looks like, if there's shootin, it's gonna be up to me and you."

Snarf didn't mind the sound of that.

They were saddled up and on their way inside an hour. The cold morning air seemed to turn hot in a flash. Poor Snarf had to lean back, with his hands propped on the rump of Redskin's horse, to get a little distance from the Indian's sweaty back.

"Hang in there. We'll get you a horse in Ithaca," DC said.

Snarf couldn't wait.

12

Ithaca began life as a trading post. It eked out a miserable living on buffalo skins and wampum for 40 years. Then the railroad came, and the railroad brought with it the world: southern cotton, northern steel, mail from everywhere, prosperity, debauchery, and noise and clamor. The buffalo and all God-fearing creatures fled and never looked back. *The railroad giveth and the railroad taketh away, blessed be the railroad* was the unwritten motto of the people of Ithaca.

In the afternoon, when Snarf and DC arrived, Ithaca was in full throb. The streets teemed. The trains screamed. And Snarf could hardly believe his eyes. He sat behind Redskin like an idiot, his mouth hanging open, his head turning this way and that, and his eyes as wide as moons.

DC led them toward The Dud Stud, which was the premiere establishment in Ithaca, not just for liquor and women, but for practically anything. It was a saloon, emporium, train station, courthouse, jail, general store, and livestock auction block all rolled into one long, sprawling building. Its history was notorious, and its future was bright, like all of America.

Snarf gaped as DC pushed open The Dud Stud's ornate batwing doors. Gas lights illuminated the few shadows left by the sunlight pouring through the great leaded windows, the polished floor would have moved Unk to tears, and an in-tune piano, that holy of holies, tinkled under its player's fat fingers.

"We don't serve their kind here," Surly Joe, the bartender announced. They had no idea what he was talking about. "Your Indian. We don't serve his kind here."

"Wait outside, will you?" DC said to Redskin. "We don't want any trouble."

Redskin left without protest.

DC put a big hand on Snarf's back and guided him toward the bar. "Now, I b'lieve it's high time I corrected a defect in your eddication." He pushed Snarf onto a barstool then boldly reached over the bar and grabbed a bottle of whisky, a bottle of water, and three small shot glasses. He winked at Surly Joe who grunted and turned his back on these uppity out-of-town self-service customers. DC slid one of the empty shot glasses to Snarf. "You had a slug of whisky before?"

"Lotsa times."

"Ok. Say that's a slug of whisky. How'd you drink it?"

Snarf grabbed the glass and pretended to toss it down his throat like he'd seen Billy and thousands of other men do and had even done himself from time to time when Unk wasn't looking.

"That's what I was afraid of. God didn't invent whisky so men'd get drunk on it. He invented it to elevate their senses. Watch." DC poured one shot glass full of water and another half full of whisky. Then he stuck his finger into the water and dripped two or three drops of it into his whisky. Then he dried his wet finger on his pant leg, lifted the whisky to his nose, rolled it around in the glass, breathed in deeply and let the air out with an, "Ahhhhhhh..." Then he poured half the shot into his mouth, closed his eyes, and rolled the stuff around in his mouth for a moment. Finally he swallowed. He kept his eyes closed while the whiskey oozed down into his stomach. Then he looked at Snarf, "Now you try."

Snarf poured himself half a shot, dripped in a few drops of water, wiped his wet finger on his pants, and lifted the whisky to his nose. It smelled like turpentine. He tried to let the air out with an 'Ahhhhh...' like DC had, but he coughed.

"Keep your mouth open when you breathe it in."

Snarf snarfed then tried again, this time with his mouth open, and didn't cough. It still smelt like turpentine, though. He poured half the shot into his mouth. It burned his tongue. He swallowed it fast and felt it move like lava down his throat and into his stomach, where it pooled and smoked. He let out a shuddery breath.

DC thumped him on the back, "Good, idn't it? And drinkin it thisa way slows you down. That's why I said any man gets drunk on whisky's doin in wrong. You remember that." This last wasn't a question, but rather a command.

Snarf nodded. He didn't like whisky anyway.

"Bottom's up," DC said and downed the rest of his shot.

Snarf, not really wanting to, did the same. His guts burned. He shivered and felt suddenly cold. He felt like the only thing in the world that could warm him up was more whisky. But DC slapped down some coin and pushed him away from the bar.

Snarf followed him into Crumpacker's General Store. Snarf knew it was Crumpacker's General Store because where the bar, poker tables, and billiard tables ended, there was a red line painted on the floor and a sign hanging from the ceiling that said, "Crumpacker's General Store."

Crossing the red line was like being transported by magic into a different world. The clattering of poker chips, the cracking of billiard balls, and the thunking of heavy glasses on heavy wooden tables ceased instantly, and the smell of leather, molasses, and pig iron washed over them.

Crumpacker himself was an institution. An old, mean, weathered man, as petulant and irascible as a willow. He'd forged his legendary emporium over decades. However, Crumpacker was not behind the counter. Instead, there was a little bearded man whose slumped shoulders were about as pronounced as the shoulders of a string bean. He was poring over a huge ledger.

"Where's Crumpacker?" DC asked.

"I am Crumpacker," the little man said. "His grandson, that is."

DC cocked an eyebrow. The idea that this weakling had sprung from the loins of a man like Crumpacker stretched credulity.

"Grandson-in-law," Little Crumpacker clarified.

That figured. "Crumpacker dead?" DC asked.

"No. No. He- he's very much alive, just indisposed at present."

"We'll wait then."

"I apologize, but it is not likely he'll be able to attend you. His age, you see, has... indisposed him."

"Indisposed," DC repeated. "I get it. Old man's sittin in a rocker listenin to the corn grow, and you moved in on him."

"Something like that," Crumpacker's grandson-in-law pushed his glasses back up nose. They tended to slide when he got nervous. He was always nervous. "How may I assist you today?"

"You can assist me, and my deputy here, with an outfit. The works. Two barrels of salt pork, rope, ground corn..." DC rattled off an extensive list while Little Crumpacker fished frantically for an order form, found it, and began scribbling down everything he could remember and everything that was being rattled off at the same time.

Once the recitation and re-recitation were complete, Little Crumpacker worked out the total. It was very large and made him very nervous. His glasses nearly slid off. "Twenty one dollars and seventy-two cents."

DC grunted. "I got fifteen dollars even."

A nervous smile twitched at the corner of Little Crumpacker's lips, "We do not negotiate at Crumpacker's-"

"Crumpacker always did."

"We're under new management." A bead of sweat ran down his temple.

"Under new management," DC said, then he looked sideways at the open ledger. "Lotta red in that book."

Little Crumpacker shut the huge ledger with a dusty thud. "Our financial information is proprietary."

"Sounds like a deal to me; you keep your financial information to yourself and I'll keep my fifteen dollars to myself," he turned away.

"Wait!" Little Crumpacker called. "I don't suppose you could do eighteen?"

"If I had eighteen dollars, I'd give it to you. But all I got is fifteen. You can take it or you can leave it."

Little Crumpacker sweated anxiously. "Fine," he said and he crossed off the original total and wrote $15 on the order form.

"Yer a wise man," DC knelt and took the wad of cash from his boot. It was instantly evident to all of them that he had a great deal more than fifteen dollars - probably a hundred and fifteen - but he only put fifteen down on the counter. The rest he stuffed in his pocket.

Little Crumpacker wiped the sweat from his brow. "Sir, that is not fair."

"Oh, I don't know about that. It was just a friendly bluff."

"My livelihood is not to be compared with a game of cards."

"It's not?"

"I say, you cheated me. I say, you lied."

DC grinned like the Cheshire Cat. "Your words have gottin smaller and less polite the longer we've talked. I wouldn't go no further if I was you, or you'll find yourself negotiatin with St. Peter, and I hear he drives a mighty hard bargain."

"You- you said you only had fifteen dollars."

"I meant I only had fifteen dollars *for you*. If you heard something else, well, I can't help what other people hear."

"We do not negotiate at Crumpacker's-"

"But you did," DC tapped the order form on the place where Little Crumpacker had scratched out the original total and written $15. "You did negotiate- not as well as ole Crumpacker hisself, but you did negotiate."

Little Crumpacker took his glasses off, cleaned them, and put them on again. This seemed to have a calming effect. "Crumpacker's thanks you for your patronage, sir."

DC tipped his hat. "And I thank you," he turned to leave- "Oh! One more thing."

Little Crumpacker fortified himself for another round.

"Need a cleaning kit for my deputy's pistol."

"A dollar fifty."

DC reached for his wad.

"We do not negotiate at Crumpacker's."

DC put two dollars on the counter. "Keep the change," he said. Then he winked at Little Crumpacker and handed the cleaning kit to Snarf.

Outside The Dud Stud, DC lit a cigarette. "Two kinds a people in this world, deputy. Those who can horse trade and those who can't."

"You think he'll be alright?"

"What d'you mean?"

"His store. You think he'll lose it?"

"Probably."

The idea hurt Snarf. He'd just lost his saloon, and it hadn't been a pleasant experience.

"Then again," DC said seeing the look in Snarf's eye, "maybe not. I taught him a valuable lesson. He takes it to heart and stands his ground from here on, he'll have a chance, maybe even thank me. Now where'd that Indian get to?" he asked, looking around for Redskin, who was nowhere to be seen.

They stood there together for a moment, shielding their eyes from the sun and looking up and down the crowded streets. Then Snarf saw a red hand go up and wave at them.

"You said Snarf needed a horse," Redskin announced as they reached him. "I believe he can find one here to suit him."

They were standing outside a corral in which a little negro boy was holding a rope and working a mare round in a circle. Along three sides of the corral, horses watched from their stalls. Snarf's eyes widened at the beautiful animals.

13

"How do I pick?" Snarf asked eagerly, looking at all the horses.

"Just find the strongest one you can get your legs round," DC said. "Him. There." He pointed at a big brown horse.

Snarf hurried to his stall. "He's huge!"

"You can sit him."

"You really think so?"

"You might have to grow a bit, but you've got some growin left in you."

Snarf looked up at the big brown horse, but the big brown horse did not look down at him. His eyes were on the mare the negro was exercising in the yard.

"Snarf," Redskin interrupted, "all horses are strong. But to trust in their strength alone is unwise. Your life may depend on your horse. And, if it does, you will want a horse that walks the Way of the Spirit."

"The Way of the Spirit?"

"Go down the line. When you meet a horse who walks the Way of the Spirit, you will know. And that horse will be the one."

DC shook his head, "The one. Never in my life..." he muttered.

But the big brown horse still had eyes only for the mare. So Snarf decided to give it a try. He went to the next horse. This one looked right at him, but with a blank animal stare. The next horse was eating with its back to him. He tried to catch its eye, but it decided to relieve itself. Snarf moved on.

The next horse was standing quietly in her pen, her gray coat speckled with white, like a starry sky in winter. She looked at him, and their eyes locked. Maybe it was the way she stood or maybe it was the tilt of her head or maybe it was something else, but Snarf knew that she was a peaceful creature and that she would take care of him.

DC whistled. "She's a looker!" he teased, breaking the spell. "Ask her to marry you, see what she says!"

Snarf was embarrassed. "I want the big one."

"Course you do."

"Are you certain?" Redskin asked.

Snarf was.

"Are you certain? Course he's certain. Good choice, deputy. Let's get him out and look him over."

DC opened the big brown horse's stall and pulled him out by the reins. He was a beautiful animal. His brown coat rippled like gold in the sun. Snarf looked up at his high back - he was gonna need a ladder just to get into the saddle.

"He's fine. Real fine." DC turned to the negro, "Hey, boy, where's the boss?"

The negro pointed to a building across the street. They went to it, DC leading the way with Redskin following and Snarf loitering along behind, feeling little next to the colossal animal. As DC tromped up the steps of the horse traders, Snarf threw a look back at the corral. He wanted to see that gray horse again. She really had been something.

Instead, he saw Jewel and her four remaining outlaws standing in the street. "DC!" he shouted.

DC and Redskin spun around.

Jewel and her crew didn't move. They already had their hands on their guns. They were ready. The people around them and between them got out of the way in a hurry.

"Give me the map," Jewel said, putting out her gloved hand like a mother expecting a naughty child to return her knitting needles.

"The map?" DC asked.

"The one the boy's carrying in that case."

"The case? That's just a drawin of a coyote. You've seen it."

Jewel smiled grimly at them, "Then why are you here?"

"You burnt the kid's saloon down. He's gotta start again."

"Don't play coy with me." Her voice was cold and deadly.

DC beamed at them, "You're not gonna gun us down in the middle of the street in broad daylight."

Jewel smiled thinly at him, "You haven't been in Ithaca long, have you?"

DC's gun flashed like a jumping trout. It boomed, and the outlaw next to Flint dropped dead. Everyone ran for cover - except Snarf, who held onto the reins of the rearing brown horse for dear life. The huge beast was trying to bolt!

Bullets whizzed past them as the outlaws fired from cover. It's interesting that men in a gun battle, trying with all their might to murder each other, instinctively avoid shooting animals. Snarf tried to draw Pap's Pistol so he could be of some use, but he needed both hands on the reins.

"What're you doin?!" DC shouted at Redskin. The Indian was walking calmly back into the corral with bullets whistling past his ears and elbows. The horses screamed and kicked at the walls of their wooden cages.

Snarf wrapped the reins around his left forearm, planted his feet firmly, and twisted Pap's Pistol with his free hand. He aimed it roughly at one of the outlaws, but now that it came to pulling the trigger, he hesitated. The man was a man, after all. More or less like himself. A little older, but made of the same stuff. Snarf found he didn't want to shoot him. Then the man cracked off a shot at DC. Snarf felt something hot spring to life inside him. His finger tightened on the trigger - the big brown horse bolted.

Snarf yelped as his arm was nearly wrenched from its socket. Then his mouth filled with dust as the big brown horse dragged him into the middle of the street, toward Jewel! Snarf let go of the reins. He rolled to a stop in a cloud of dust. He was alone and much closer to Jewel and the outlaws than he was to DC.

Jewel came at him, derringer raised, her outlaws blasting away at DC to keep him pinned down.

"Snarf!" DC shouted, unable to do anything.

"Give it to me," Jewel demanded.

Snarf felt for Pap's Pistol, but it'd been wrenched from his belt when he was dragged. He clutched the map case and shook his head. She'd have to kill him first, but killing was alright with Jewel. She raised her derringer.

Inside the corral, Redskin was at the gray mare's stall. Despite the din of the panicking horses all around her, she was an oasis of calm. Redskin opened her stall. It rattled as she shot out of it.

Jewel cocked her derringer - her gloved finger tightened on the trigger. The tiny barrel filled Snarf's vision. The gray horse smashed into the derringer from the side. It fired once, wildly into the air, then flew out of her hand. Jewel herself sprawled in the road.

The gray horse loomed over her, her neck erect, her nostrils wide, her mane blowing in the wind like fire, and her eyes raging at the dusty woman lying within striking distance of her hooves.

Jewel froze.

Her outlaws stopped shooting.

DC peeped out from his cover, which had nearly been chewed out of existence by the outlaws' bullets.

Stunned by the miraculous appearance of the gray horse, Snarf watched Jewel slowly climb to her feet. Her hair was disordered, her dress dusty, and her eyes wild with rage, but she had no weapons. The gray horse glared at her. Jewel turned slowly away and walked back toward her outlaw companions. Feeling the horse's hot eyes on her back, Jewel's walk became a run. "Go!" she screamed.

The gray horse charged at her with murderous intent. Thankfully for Jewel, Flint had made for their horses. He rode at her now and swooped her up into the saddle just before the gray horse chased her down. They turned and raced out of Ithaca, with the two surviving outlaws following close behind.

"You ok?" DC asked as he reached Snarf.

"Yeah," Snarf said. DC helped him up. They watched the gray horse give up the chase. She reared and neighed at the fleeing outlaws, declaring that if they ever tried anything like that again, they'd have her to reckon with. Redskin joined them. They all watched the gray horse walk back toward them. She was a gorgeous animal.

"I, uh, I don't see that big brown horse anywhere. Do you?" DC asked.

Snarf sure didn't. The big brown horse was long gone.

"She walks the Way of the Spirit," Redskin said as the gray horse reached them. "Choose her and you choose wisely."

The gray horse lowered her head so she was eye to eye with Snarf. She had a little nick on her shoulder where the bullet from Jewel's derringer had grazed her. Snarf put a hand on her hot nose. She pressed forward and put her head on his shoulder. He wrapped his arms around her strong neck. They stayed like that for a moment, the boy and the gray horse, while their hearts knitted themselves together.

"I hate to interrupt the matrimony or whatever it is you're doin," DC said, "but we gotta problem.

"Our one advantage over Craney was the element of surprise. Seems as we've lost that," he said, looking at the cloud of dust thrown up by the fleeing outlaws. "So, unless we mean to kill our horses in hot pursuit, Craney's gonna know we're comin."

"We could hire some men - form a posse?" Snarf suggested.

DC didn't like that idea. "A posse. Every posse I ever been a part of, someone always turns traitor. Always."

"Then what do you suggest?" Redskin asked.

A train whistle blew.

DC smiled at the sound.

14

At a fairground, perhaps, or at some old out-of-the-way museum with blocked gutters, you may have seen a steam locomotive in action. If so, you know that "seen" is not the word. It is heard: the roar, metal-scream, deep bellow of the huge black monster! Yes, and even then it is only a locomotive you are thinking of, not an entire train. Imagine it now, the wheels nearly as tall as you, forged of heavy steel, and balanced on just two and a half inches of rail. Add the booming chug of the hot pistons to the musical wail of the whistle. Add cars packed with people, animals, goods, and weapons as far as you can see, like some endless snake. Now the smoke billows, black and heavy. The driving wheels turn - slip! - catch. The cars lurch, banging together, making thunder. The earth rumbles under the weight of all those elements - steel, fire, water, iron, copper, wood, tar, and coal congealed into one unstoppable mass - hurtling, driving, louder than Niagara, heavier than a mountain.

Now you understand why the buffalo and all God-fearing creatures fled.

Snarf put his head out the window of their train car. The

wind mussed his hair and tried to tear his shirt off. What a sight it was to see the rocks beneath him rushing by like white water, while the hills far away rolled gently past.

"Look!" Snarf shouted.

DC and Redskin pressed their faces to the window. There, out in the desert, they saw Jewel and Flint and the two surviving outlaws trotting along.

DC sprang to his feet and threw open his window. He cupped his hands to his mouth and hollered, "Watch out for coyotes!"

Snarf threw his head back and howled. Flint drew his pistol, but Jewel stayed him with a hand. The outlaws watched helplessly as the train outran them.

Snarf and DC slammed their windows shut and slumped into their seats. Grinning like fools, they stuffed their mussed hair back into their hats.

"That was most improvident," Redskin said.

"Improvident. Where'd you get all your fancy words, Redskin?" DC asked.

"At school."

What school Redskin had been to, DC couldn't imagine. "At school," he repeated. "What are they gonna do? Fly to Craney?"

Snarf laughed. Redskin cut his laugh short by glaring at him. Snarf snarfed.

"Come with me," Redskin said, standing. "We need to tend your horse."

Snarf turned to DC. The idea of being alone with the Indian made him nervous, but DC gave him a little nod. Reluctantly, he went with Redskin.

The stable car smelt of straw and horse intermingled with the occasional draft of fresh air that snuck through the gaps in the wallboards. Snarf followed Redskin cautiously down the narrow aisle that ran along the stables.

"My horse's name is Beautiful Feet," Redskin announced as they passed him.

"He's beautiful all right," Snarf said.

"What is your name?"

Snarf gave Redskin a funny look. "Snarf," he said, and he gave a demonstration.

"Your real name."

"It's Snarf. My last name's Bridges. My parents died before they gave me a real name, and Unk never called me anything other."

"Then you must choose a name for yourself."

"Why?"

"Because your name defines you. If your name is Snarf, that is all you are, to others and to yourself. It is possible that is all you will become: a snarf."

"Did you choose your name?" Snarf asked, expecting to catch the Indian in a contradiction.

"I did."

Snarf was surprised, "Well, if your name defines you, you chose a bad one. Who'd want to be thought of as a redskin?" As soon as the words left his mouth, he realized his mistake. His cheeks reddened. "I meant-"

Redskin held up a hand to stop his excuse. "You asked an honest question, there is no fault in that. "I chose the name Redskin for many reasons. One you just mentioned; because men think little of me, it is easier for me to move among them unnoticed or at least unharmed. If my name were Black Elk, do you think I would have survived my sudden appearance in your town?"

Snarf could see the point.

"Some may accuse me of cowardice for such a choice, but I put little stock in the accusations of those who do not know me. Also, I chose the name Redskin because the first man and the first woman were made out of clay as red as the reddest blood, or so many of my people believe. And I chose my name to honor the Son of the Great Father, whose skin turned red with blood before he gave up his spirit."

"Has your skin ever turned red?"

"Some would say it is red now."

"You know what I mean - with blood?"

"No. I have not yet resisted to the point of shedding blood."

"Resisted what?"

"My flesh," Redskin answered. Then he returned to his original point because they had reached the gray horse's stall. "Someday, Snarf, you will have to choose a name for yourself; but, today, you must choose a name for your horse."

"Mary Beth," Snarf's answer came fast and sure. "It was my mother's name."

"It is a good name and well suited."

Mary Beth put her head out of the stall, and Redskin patted her. She was a fine creature. While she smelled Snarf's hand, Redskin inspected the graze on her shoulder. It was not dangerous. It would heal.

"You said, back in Ithaca, that Mary Beth walks the Way of the Spirit. What'd you mean?"

"There are only two ways through life; the Way of the Flesh and the Way of the Spirit. All men are born Fleshwalkers; their strength is their strength, and they use it to get whatever they want. Sometimes this looks good, like a man going about his work, earning an honest living, building a home. Sometimes it looks bad, like a man stealing or killing. But, whether it looks good or bad, whether a man's body is weak or strong, whether he is lazy or a warrior, no man can ever satisfy his flesh. His god is his belly, his mouth is an open grave, his end is death, and his ravenous soul will spend its forever life in famished torment, weeping and gnashing its teeth because the Great Father cannot tolerate Fleshwalkers."

"Is that true?" Snarf asked because it sounded pretty awful.

"It is half of the truth. The other half is this: the Son of the Great Father opened the Way of the Spirit to us. He was the first Spiritwalker. However, we Fleshwalkers could not tolerate him. His very existence condemned us, his every word pierced us, and his every action defied us, until we could stand it no longer. We threw him out. We shunned him and drove him away until he had no place to lay his head and no tribe to call his own. Then, when even that did not satisfy us, we killed him." Redskin smiled at Snarf, who did not understand how anything he'd just said could possibly prompt a smile. "But we Fleshwalkers were fools. We did not know that it is impossible to kill a Spiritwalker."

"What d'you mean?"

"The Son of the Great Father returned to life and, in so doing, he opened the Way of the Spirit to all."

"You killed him, and he came back to life? That's impossible."

"For a Fleshwalker like you, it is."

"You mean, if I walk the Way of the Spirit, if I become a Spiritwalker, I can die and come back to life?"

"To become a Spiritwalker is to die and be born again."

"That's crazy."

"It only seems crazy because you walk the Way of the Flesh."

"Let's say I wanted to become a Spiritwalker, so I could die and come back to life, how would I do it?"

"The Son of the Great Father said it is easier for a buffalo to go through the eye of a needle than it is for a man to become a Spiritwalker. What do you think would happen to a buffalo if it went through the eye of a needle?"

Snarf shrugged, "I dunno."

"It would die. The needle would scrape off all its skin."

Snarf shuddered at the thought.

"And so you cannot choose to become a Spiritwalker because you, like the buffalo, cannot go through the eye of a needle. The Great Father must choose you. And if he does, you will not be able to resist him. He will kill your flesh and cause you to be born again. Then, and only then, will you be a Spiritwalker." Redskin turned to leave.

"But that doesn't make any sense," Snarf said.

"He who has ears to hear, let him hear."

"I have ears!" Snarf shouted after him. "I have ears, but it doesn't make any sense!"

Redskin shut the door behind himself, leaving Snarf alone with Mary Beth.

15

The full moon shone down brightly on heliograph station 15. Perched on a hilltop, the station consisted of a large tent from which came the soft sounds of sleeping men, a fire pit, very ashy because the men always bickered about whose turn it was to clean it, and the heliograph itself, a simple box-like thing on a tripod. There was also a desolate guard patrolling the empty space between the tent and the dying fire. He and his unhappy shadow stopped their parade to watch a distant train steaming through the desert. From this far away, the locomotive sounded like a waterfall, a steady consistent thunder.

Suddenly, the guard heard a horse galloping toward him. Before he could sling his rifle from his shoulder, Jewel burst out of the night and threw herself into his arms. When their bodies made contact, the guard was certain he had fallen asleep and was dreaming. He was not anxious to waken.

"Please!" Jewel cried, "Please, you've got to help me! There are three of them!"

"Three what?"

"Men!" she shrieked, stabbing her finger back into the darkness while she scrambled to get behind her savior.

The guard unslung his rifle and pointed it into the night. "Up, boys! Trouble!" he yelled toward the tent, but they had already heard. Two more guards fell out almost instantly, big men with rifles ready. Behind them came a pair of men with pistols. These two looked frightened and they were still blinking the sleep out of their eyes and fumbling with their spectacles. They all pointed their guns into the night and strained to see the oncoming danger.

"There were three of them," Jewel cried. "They've chased me for miles."

"I don't see nothin."

"Oh, please, don't let them..." Jewel whimpered. She cast a surreptitious glance backward and saw Flint and her other two outlaws oozing out of the darkness. They had their pistols drawn and pointed at the backs of the soldiers. She put up her hand for them to wait. She went to one of the men with spectacles, spun him around, and kissed him hard on the mouth. While she kissed him, she dragged him out of the firing line and took the pistol out of his hand. He did not resist.

Seeing Jewel kissing his companion, one of the soldiers asked, "What the-?" But it was too late. Flint and the others opened fire.

The man broke away from Jewel, surprise, betrayal, and disappointment on his face. Jewel leveled his pistol at his chest. "I need to send a message," she said. "Is that possible?"

"Yes."

They looked at each other for a moment. He was going to make her command his every move. That was fine with her. "Please, ready the instrument," she ordered.

The man went to the heliograph, checked the position of the moon, and made some adjustments. Finished, he asked, "What's the message?"

She smiled. "Why do men always think beautiful women are stupid?"

"I don't-" but a bullet tore out his heart.

Jewel tossed his smoking gun into the darkness after him then went to the heliograph. She depressed a lever on its side, and a little window snapped open, revealing a mirror shining with moonlight.

After a short wait, an answering flash came from a faraway hilltop. Jewel worked her lever, sending a Morse Code message across the desert at light-speed.

Between the two hilltops, the train chugged slowly along.

DC and Redskin were asleep in the train, but not Snarf. He was awake in his bed under DC's bunk, the bottom of which was so close to his face that he was sure if he stuck his tongue out, he'd be able to lick it. He felt like he was breathing the same air over and over again.

Then DC's bunk began to descend toward him. It was coming slowly, but it was coming closer... and closer...

Snarf jumped out of bed. He was sweating. And he felt silly because DC's bed hadn't moved an inch. It had just been a trick played on him by his mind. He didn't like tight spaces. And no wonder, he was from the desert where there are no tight spaces.

He went to the window and watched the vast empty land roll by. He thought about what Redskin had said about the Way of the Flesh. It sounded an awful lot like what Billy'd called the Ecstasy of Gold.

Snarf sat up because a man had appeared in the desert. He was far away and tiny, but his shadow, cast by the full moon, was long and grim. He seemed to be watching the train. Really, Snarf thought, the man was looking right at him, even though he was too far away to see the man's face, and the man couldn't possibly see him in the darkness of the moving train car. He hoped.

The man raised his left arm, pointing at something. Snarf

followed the direction of the man's finger. A hilltop. Wait! There was a light flashing on the hilltop.

Snarf looked back at the man. He put his left arm down and pointed with his right. Snarf followed that one to another hilltop and another flashing light! He looked back at the man, but the man was gone.

"DC!" Snarf shouted.

DC lurched out of bed, pistol ready.

"DC, look!" Snarf pointed at the flashing hilltops.

DC squinted at the lights. "Heliographs. Never seen em work at night before."

"There was a man in the desert. He pointed at them, then he was gone."

"A man?"

"Yeah, he was right there," Snarf pointed at the place, but there was no one there and no sign anyone ever had been there.

"Right there. First Redskin, now you," DC said, yawning. "Next thing you know, I'm gonna be givin my Christmas list to St. Nic hisself. Maybe I'll get what I want for a change, cut out the middle man." He slid down into his bedroll and closed his eyes.

Snarf looked at Redskin. The Indian was watching him intently from the darkness of his bunk. Snarf didn't like the comparison between himself and the crazy Indian. He lay down and put his back to Redskin. Eventually he fell asleep.

16

When Snarf finally woke, the train car was hot and stuffy with sunlight. He peeled off his covers and sat up, blinking his dry eyes and snarfing. DC was gone, but Redskin was still watching him. Snarf froze. The Indian had his big golden book open in his lap. He'd been reading. And waiting.

"What d'you want?" Snarf asked.

"Tell me about the man you saw in the desert," Redskin said, closing his book.

"No thanks," Snarf replied as he headed for the door.

"You may not have ears to hear, but it seems you have eyes to see."

Snarf stopped. He didn't like the idea that he was seeing things, but he was curious. One second the man had been there, then he'd been gone. Just like that. Granted, it had been very dark, so maybe he hadn't seen anything, but he didn't really believe that. He sat back down. "You think I saw what-ever whoever it is you see?"

Redskin nodded.

"Do you see him now?"

"Yes."

"Where?"

"There," Redskin pointed to the empty spot by the window just beside Snarf.

There was, of course, no one there, but the space *was* big enough that a man could - *could* - be sitting there. "What's he look like?" Snarf asked, hardly believing he was even asking the question.

"He is thin and wiry with strength, like a man who has spent his life in the desert. He has a dark, very dark, beard, cut close. His eyes are dark also. I do not think he slept much while he was alive, but his eyes are calm; they are the eyes of a man who knows he will win any contest. His forehead is marred by many scars and adorned with a band of golden beads. He wears a woven red poncho over buckskins."

Snarf shook his head, "He wasn't an Indian. The man I saw was wearing a hat, like mine."

"I did not say he was an Indian. I described his dress, which he may change."

"Who is he?"

"He is the Son of the Great Father."

"And you think I saw him last night?"

"Don't you?"

Snarf didn't want to answer that question because to give an answer either way would have felt like a commitment of some kind.

"If it was him," Redskin said, "then it is possible you have been chosen to become a Spiritwalker."

"What if I don't wanna be a Spiritwalker?"

"That is your choice."

"Yesterday you said I didn't have a choice."

"You do not."

The contradiction hung in the air between them, awaiting

an explanation. "If you are chosen, you will choose. If you are not chosen, you will not choose," Redskin explained.

"What if I'm chosen, but choose not to choose?"

"Impossible."

"Then I don't really chose- in the end, I mean. It's just fate. I don't have to do anything. I'm either chosen or not chosen, wait and see."

Redskin smiled, "You are very clever."

"I think so."

"But you do not understand." He gave Snarf a moment to get over his frank statement before asking, "Have you ever been in love?"

Snarf shook his head and blushed and thought of Jewel's gloved hands.

"Being chosen to become a Spiritwalker is like falling in love. You meet someone and your heart begins to pound, your cheeks flush."

Snarf snarfed, hoping to wipe the blush off his cheeks. It didn't work.

"Your every waking thought is about her and her alone. Eventually, you ask her to marry you, and she says yes. You chose her, did you not? So, what if she knew you were going to fall in love with her? What if, the first time you saw her, she had put herself in front of you because she knew you were the one for her and she was the one for you and if she stood in just that place, you would see her and fall in love with her. Did you choose her then?"

Snarf cleared his throat of the stuff that had collected there while he'd thought of Jewel. "I guess so," he said.

"And so I say again, if you are chosen, you will choose. If you are not chosen, you will not choose. You have no choice."

"How?"

"How what?"

"How do I choose or not choose?"

"If you are chosen, you must do two things. First, you will see the Son of the Great Father as I do, as a great Chief, a warrior whom you would follow into any battle, even one you know will cost you your life. Second, you must kill your flesh."

Snarf frowned, "If I kill my flesh, won't I be dead?"

"Your flesh is not your body. Your flesh is that part of you that wants."

"Wants what?"

"Anything. Strength, power, gold, comfort, food, women, water, a family, anything other than the Great Father and his Son."

"The Ecstasy of Gold," Snarf offered.

Redskin nodded.

"What if I can't? What if I can't stop wanting?"

"Ah, very good. You are clever and wise. You are right; you cannot stop wanting. However, at the moment the Son of the Great Father appears glorious to you, he will kill your flesh."

"You just said–"

"He will kill your flesh, but your flesh will still be alive, like a shadow cast by fire." His eyes burned with zeal. "You," he poked Snarf in the chest, "*you* must kill your flesh." Then he blinked and suddenly, he wasn't looking at Snarf anymore. He was looking inside himself. "Or it will kill you," he said, his voice barely a whisper. Then he leaned back, into the shadow of his bunk.

Snarf felt as if Redskin had forgotten he was there. He didn't know what to say or do while the Indian sat under the darkness of the bunk, silently looking at something inside himself. Thankfully, the door to their train car slid open. It was DC. "Breakfast time," he announced.

Snarf hopped to his feet and pushed quickly past the sheriff. DC looked at Redskin for an explanation, but the Indian was as inscrutable as ever, so DC went to breakfast. He was hungry.

Redskin sat alone, looking at the place he had told Snarf the Son of the Great Father was sitting. He looked for a long time.

17

Since Snarf had spent his life as the only cook in The Six, the idea of someone else preparing his food for him was exciting in the extreme. After the waiter sat them at a table in the dining car, Snarf watched him disappear into the kitchen. As the door swung open, he caught a glimpse of the sweaty negroes making their food.

"Over there," DC said, nudging Snarf to sit on the other side of the booth. "If you're next to me, I can't get my gun out."

"What do we need our guns for?" Snarf asked, looking around nervously. Then he saw a group of four soldiers, with uniforms very like the ones worn by Flint and Craney's other outlaws, sitting at a nearby table.

"I dunno," DC said, his eyes flicking away from the soldiers, "but I don't aim to get shot before I got breakfast in me." DC snapped his napkin into his lap.

Snarf imitated the action.

"What were you and Redskin jawin about?"

"He was tellin me how to be a Spiritwalker."

"A Spiritwalker?" DC asked, then he decided he didn't want

to know. "Look, there's only two kinds a injun religion. The Kumbaya, sister moon, brother son kind - but you don't hear much about them anymore cause they're mostly dead - and the scalpin kind that we're still dealin with.

"Now our redskin's obviously the peaceful type, which is fine with me, and good luck too cause I can sleep at night, but I don't need you convertin on me. Besides you're white, and I never heard of such a thing as a white man takin up a red man's religion. No, you stick to Christ and Him crucified and all that stuff, you hear me?"

Snarf, feeling chastised, nodded. The waiter arrived.

"Flapjacks," DC said, "Double the syrup and double the bacon."

"Yes, sir."

"Scrambled eggs, please," Snarf said.

The waiter headed for the kitchen. Snarf leaned out, hoping to catch another glimpse of the cooks at work, but Redskin arrived. Snarf moved into the booth, to make room, and as he did, he noticed all four of the soldiers at the nearby table were looking at them.

"DC," Snarf said, trying to act cool, "you see the soldiers over there."

"Yeah, I seen em."

"Are they still lookin at us?"

"At us? No."

"They were. All four of em."

"What is the matter?" Redskin asked.

"Think they're Craney's?" Snarf whispered.

"Just cause they got uniform-" DC shut up because all four of the soldiers were standing up. "Oh, boy," he said. The soldiers came toward them.

Under the table, DC slipped his pistol out of its black holster. Snarf put his hand on Pap's Pistol and twisted it up at the men. Redskin felt the movement. Without taking his eyes off the oncoming soldiers, he pulled Snarf's hand off the pistol. Snarf glanced at Redskin, but the Indian's eyes were fixed on the soldiers.

The leader, a square-jawed hero type, stood over them. "Are you three going after the deserter and outlaw Matthew Craney?"

"Nope," DC lied.

"The truth," Redskin interjected, "may serve us better."

"The truth," DC glared at the Indian.

"Craney killed my uncle and burned down my saloon," Snarf explained, now that the cat was out of the bag.

"Your saloon?" one of the soldiers asked, wondering at Snarf's youth.

But the square-jawed soldier understood; they were after justice. "You see the heliograph's flashing last night?" he asked.

DC nodded, "We seen em."

"Read it," the square-jawed soldier ordered one of his compatriots.

The soldier produced a slip of paper and read from it, "Man, boy, Indian coming by rail. Stop. They know location of gold. Stop. Be ready, Craney. Stop."

"Thought you ought to know what you're walking into," the square-jawed soldier said, then he tipped his hat and led his men back to their table.

"Wait!" Snarf called. "Did you happen to see a man in the desert? He was between the two hills," Snarf explained. "He pointed at the helio-" Snarf couldn't pronounce it, "at the lights."

The soldiers looked at each other. None of them had seen a man in the desert. "Sorry, kid," the square-jawed leader said. They went back to their table.

Snarf felt very foolish.

"Craney knows we're comin," DC muttered. He slammed the table, making the glasses and silverware rattle. Just then the waiter passed. DC grabbed his arm, "How long till we get to the station?"

"We're almost there, sir."

"Almost - how long?"

"Half an hour. No more."

DC released him. "C'mon," he said, climbing out of the booth.

"What about breakfast?" Snarf asked.

"No breakfast today," DC growled, leading them out of the dining car.

18

DC swung the hinged table down from the wall of their train car. Then he fished out the pistol cleaning kit they'd bought in Ithaca. "Get out your pepperbox," he ordered Snarf.

Snarf put Pap's pistol on the table. Fine black powder coated its barrels. "You think Craney's gonna be at the station?" he asked.

"Don't you?"

Snarf did, and it frightened him. All the fights he'd been in so far had been ambushes. He'd never walked into one on purpose. And even then, he hadn't been able to fire at that outlaw in Ithaca until he got riled up.

DC fiddled with Pap's Pistol. Grit stymied the rotating barrels, and ancient grease gummed the trigger. "Yer gun is your most valuable tool," he said as he disassembled the weapon. "Without it, you're just a decorated sodbuster." He flicked his sheriff's badge, making it ring. "So keep it clean. You get in a fracas with some nasty barves, spend half a night rollin in the mud and half a day sweatin like a mule, you clean your gun before you wash your face. You clean your gun before you eat. You clean your gun before you sleep. You clean your gun before you press."

Snarf giggled.

"Don't laugh. Dyin on the press's an ugly way to go. I seen it. More'n once." DC scoured the barrels with a wire brush while Snarf bit his lip to keep from laughing.

"I can see the station," Redskin said from the corner where he'd squeezed himself.

Snarf joined him and, sure enough, there was the station on the horizon. People teemed on the platform. Any one of them might be Craney...

"Sheriff," Redskin said, "we have lost the element of surprise. Is it wise to go on?"

"Is it wise? Listen, deputy," DC declared, "justice ain't like the sun, comin up every mornin whether it feels like it or not and shinin willy-nilly, but more or less equal, on everybody. No, justice is like... well, it's like breakfast; if you don't make it, you don't have it."

"He is right," Redskin said, "bringing justice belongs to the Way of the Spirit."

"Even if you have to fight?" Snarf asked.

"Even if you have to fight," Redskin answered.

"Then why won't you?"

"We could use you," DC added.

Redskin looked at Pap's Pistol and, even though he'd never held or fired it or even seen it fired before, he knew things about it. He knew the things about Pap's Pistol that an engineer might know about a locomotive after just a glance or a blacksmith might know about a piece of metal after just a touch or a priest might know about a sinner after just a prayer. He knew exactly what Pap's Pistol would feel like as it bucked in his hand and sent one of its burning slugs into the heart of some- "You think I do not want to fight. You are wrong. I want to fight. I want to fight more than anything. And that is why I will not." With an effort, he turned his attention back to the window. "I must kill my flesh. I must earn my name."

"Your flesh?" DC asked.

"Your flesh is–" Snarf started to explain.

"Forget it," DC said. He snapped Pap's Pistol back together and handed it to Snarf. It gleamed, the trigger pulled cleanly, and the barrels rotated freely.

"Thanks," Snarf said.

DC pushed the bullets toward him then took a handful more from his gunbelt. "Load her and stuff the rest in your pockets."

"They won't go off?"

"Go off? They're bullets, not dynamite. You'll be fine."

Snarf tried to load his pistol, but his hands were shaking. He was frightened. He felt eyes on him. Redskin was watching. "The train's rocking," he explained weakly.

"Fear belongs to the Way of the Flesh."

"All your knowledge of all these various ways, it's no wonder you know where the coyote is," DC said. "I bet if someone cracked your head open, they'd find a map in there and nothin else."

The train lurched. Out their window, an ocean of people stood on the platform.

"First we get the horses," DC said, "then we get outta here. You see anyone that looks like Craney, you holler. If he's got his gun out, you shoot."

"In the crowd?" Redskin asked.

"In the crowd," DC confirmed, his eyes hard. "C'mon." He tossed his huge bedroll onto his shoulder and led them out of the train car.

19

The people getting off the train and the people getting on the train crashed together like serfs on some pointless medieval battlefield. And, like the serfs, they found themselves so pressed and pinned together that they couldn't move. They were like sardines in a can: sweaty, salty, and stuck.

"Clamp your hands on that thing," DC said, pointing at the case dangling at Snarf's hip, "or a pickpocket will take it off you like that," he snapped his fingers. Then he hopped into the sea of people. Redskin dove in after him. Snarf obediently clamped his hands over the case and plunged in too.

If not for DC's bedroll bobbing atop the surf of scalps, Snarf would have been left behind and crushed to death by the unending waves of people, but he kept his eyes on the floating mass and swam manfully on.

He did not see the round black hat turn to follow him.

Because they were headed for the rear of the train and not trying to get on or off of it, they were able to make progress through the crowd. Very little progress, but progress nonetheless. And, because they were headed for the rear of the train and not trying to get on or off of it, the man, the Indian, and the boy stood out.

The owner of the round black hat, a ratty man with a pinched face and splotchy black whiskers, saw that he was at the tail of the notorious trio and doubled his pace.

Snarf felt that prickly sensation at the back of his neck that always comes with being watched. He risked a glance backward, but saw no one - well, he saw hundreds of people, but not the man with the round black hat because he'd turned to face the train like all those waiting to board, and so, he was invisible.

Redskin and DC were quite out of range now. Snarf's heart pounded as he pushed after them. The round black hat followed, closing on its prey.

Snarf wanted to run. The heat of the sun and the people; they stank. He couldn't breathe. He couldn't see. He could barely move. He was drowning. "DC!" he shouted, but no one heard him.

A silver knife came out of the black pocket of the man with the round hat. He knew just the place in the boy's back to put the blade. The boy would not scream when the blade slid into him because the place he was going to put the knife made screaming impossible. Indeed, it made living impossible. In the knife would go, down the boy would go, and off he would go with the map to Craney. No one would notice the body until the train left the station.

Snarf saw the man and the knife. The world lurched under him, his stomach heaved, his ears roared, and the blood rushed to his legs, lending them wild, irresistible impetus. He spun and pushed frantically into the people. Some gave way, some cursed, a woman yelped when he stepped on her foot.

DC whipped around. He saw Snarf, and he saw the man with the black hat closing on him. "Snarf!" He dropped his bedroll and drew his pistol, but there were too many people in the way. There was no clean shot, and when it came to it, he really couldn't bring himself to fire into the crowd.

Redskin turned too. And it was a very, very providential thing for the rat-faced man, for everyone between him and Redskin, and for Redskin himself, that he was not armed, for he would not have hesitated to fire.

The knife sailed toward Snarf's back.

Snarf, driven by some wild animal instinct, spun around. He saw the knife coming at him like a lightning bolt. He raised the case like a shield. He felt the blade slash across the back of his left hand. It hardly hurt at all. Then the air hit the wound and the pain came. He screamed. He screamed because the blade was coming down again.

A hand seized the wrist holding the knife and twisted it. The wrist popped. The knife clattered to the ground. The rat-faced man shrieked and writhed against the strong arm winding its way around his neck like a python.

Snarf watched, open mouthed, as the four soldiers from the train descended on the wannabe murderer.

"Go on!" the square-jawed commander, who had the ratty man in a headlock, ordered. "Get outta here!"

Snarf didn't have to be told twice. Still clutching the case, he turned and ran. The crowd gave him a wide berth, afraid that whatever it was about him that had nearly gotten him murdered in broad daylight might somehow rub off on them.

He crashed into DC and the big man wrapped his arms around him. DC felt the boy shaking, so he squeezed him until he couldn't shake any more. Somehow that helped.

Redskin finally reached them. He'd had a tough time fighting his way through the fleeing masses, but he was there now and he was seeing red. He yanked Snarf out of DC's arms and felt him all over for stab wounds.

"He just got my hand," Snarf insisted, trying to get away

from Redskin's pawing touch so he could snarf away some embarrassing tears.

"Let me see it," Redskin pulled Snarf's hand close.

The pull hurt. "Ow!" Snarf protested, but Redskin was already fishing in his pack.

"You should have stayed close to DC," he said as he poured water over the wound.

"I tried, but there were too many people."

"Then he should have waited for you."

"Hey! I'm right here," DC reminded him.

"I said on the train we should turn back, but you would not listen. Now look," Redskin said as he bound Snarf's hand with a white handkerchief. He bound it tight.

"*I* wouldn't listen! You're losin your bonkers over a scratch, Redskin. Give him some air. Give him some air, or I'm liable to get cusstrated. I said, give him some air!" DC cried as he pulled Snarf away from Redskin. "Lawsy! What would the son of the whoever say if he saw you now?"

Redskin stood there, humiliated, with an ocean of eyes on him. He hadn't been mad at DC or Snarf or even the assassin. No, he'd been mad at himself, at what he'd almost done, at what he would have done if he'd had a gun.

Snarf saw that he'd bled all over DC's black shirtfront. "Sorry," he said.

DC looked at his blood-smeared chest and smiled wryly, "Sorry. Why do you think I wear black?"

Snarf snarfed and managed a smile.

"He get the coyote?"

Snarf shook his head and lifted the case.

"C'mon," DC said, urging Snarf out of the crowd.

Snarf looked up at Redskin, whose eyes were on the ground. "You ok?" he asked.

"You ok? Course he's ok," DC said, pulling him away from the Indian and toward the stable car where their horses and the donkey were being unloaded. "He ain't the one almost got spitted. You're gonna have a nasty scar and a story to go with it."

Snarf agreed, but he wasn't sure it was worth it. He tried flexing his hand. It hurt. Bad.

"It'll hurt worse tomorrow," DC said, "then it'll feel better. Or it'll fall off." Snarf looked at him sharply. He winked.

They really did look every bit like a father and son. Redskin trudged after them.

"Ever saddle a horse before?" DC asked.

Snarf shook his head.

"Well, there's a first time for everything, and today's one to put in the diary: got in my first knife fight and saddled my first horse." He thrust Snarf's new saddle into his arms. "Chuck it up here." He patted Mary Beth's back.

Snarf hoisted the saddle onto Mary Beth. The cut on his hand stung. He had to bite back a hiss, but he didn't want DC to think he was just a kid. He felt a little embarrassed to think about the way he'd just pressed himself, like a baby, into the big man.

"Now tighten the girth."

Snarf grabbed the girth strap with his good hand and fastened it.

"No, no, no," DC said, "too loose. The saddle'll fall right off."

"I don't want to hurt her."

"Hurt her? She can take it," DC cinched the girth tight.

Too tight in Snarf's estimation. "It don't hurt?" he asked.

"Nah. She's tough. Besides, you know what'd hurt her? You falling off," DC said, and it was evident in his eyes that it would hurt him just as much. Or more. "Get up."

Snarf climbed into the saddle.

"Feels good, don't it?"

"Sure does," Snarf said. And it did. Something about being

taller than everyone, out of the crowd, and in the fresh air, made him feel great.

Redskin appeared with Beautiful Feet. He looked up at Snarf and DC, who'd mounted Boss. "Forgive me," he said.

"Sure," DC said. "We forgive-"

"I was not finished."

DC shut his mouth.

Redskin looked Snarf in the eye. "I was afraid, and that made me ungentle. I hurt you. Will you forgive me?"

No one had ever asked Snarf such a question in his life. He had no idea what to say, so he just nodded.

"I need to hear you say it."

"Sure."

"Do you forgive me, yes or no?"

"Yeah, I forgive you."

"Thank you," Redskin said.

"Mighty big of you Red-"

"Sheriff," Redskin interrupted him, "I question the wisdom of pressing on, but I should not have blamed you for what happened. It was not your fault. Will you forgive me?"

"Yeah."

"Thank you." Ready to go, Redskin climbed on to Mary Beth but both DC and Snarf were staring at him like he was a three-legged dog.

Finally, DC cleared his throat. "We ain't payin you a hundred dollars to sit there and stare at us. C'mon, show us the way."

So Redskin did.

20

Snarf had spent his whole life in the desert, so his first sight of the vast open prairie of the Colorado Territory took his breath away. As far as he could see, there was nothing but blue sky and green grass. The earth itself was perfectly flat, like the bottom of his cast iron skillet. The wind teased his hair. He felt like the world had her arms opened wide to him. He could tell that Mary Beth felt the same. She had a spring in her step and a twinkle in her eye. He leaned down and whispered in her ear, "Wanna run?"

She burst into a gallop.

Snarf beamedas the prairie throbbed and surged beneath him. The grass went "ssshhhhhh" as it rushed past. The wind laughed in his ears. Mary Beth's mane tickled his face.

He heard thunder to his left, and there was DC galloping beside him. He had his hat in his hand and was using it urge Boss on. Then Redskin and Beatiful Feet appeared on his right. Redskin threw his head back and whooped. Snarf grinned from ear to ear. The trio galloped over the plain, the hoofbeats of their horses drumming in perfect rhythm.

Eventually, they stopped. Mary Beth's sides heaved under

Snarf. He patted her flank, and she bobbed her head in thanks. DC put his hat on Boss, and he whinnied in protest. They all laughed.

Riding over the plain was easy, and they made good progress. When they slept, the coyotes howled, but their dreams were not disturbed, probably because their bellies were so full. With Snarf as cook, they ate well.

Redskin kept the cut on the back of Snarf's hand clean and rubbed it with plants he found on the prairie. Soon, it felt better. And it didn't fall off. In fact, a bright red scar formed and that made Snarf feel like the toughest barve that ever was.

Eventually, they came to a river. It sparkled like silver through the grass. Snarf could see the fish in it. DC said they were trout and caught some to prove it. Because Snarf had never cooked fish, much less eaten it, the sheriff took his turn as cook. Snarf loved the soft, light meat. With his belly full, the prairie sky twinkling with stars, his hand marked by glory, and the nearby river singing its forever song, Snarf slept like a baby.

But he woke before dawn with DC's hand clamped over his mouth. Snarf didn't move; he just opened his eyes. The sheriff put a finger to his lips. Snarf understood he wasn't to make a sound. DC pointed.

A line of Indian warriors stood on the opposite side of the river. They prickled with spears, bows, and rifles.

Snarf shivered.

The waning moonlight danced in the river between them, and that's how Snarf saw Redskin. He was wading through the moonlight, heading toward the war party, just a silhouette in the shining water. He stopped and exchanged some words in a language neither Snarf nor DC understood. Then he took off his shirt.

"What's he doin?" Snarf whispered.

"Doin? Showin em he's a Indian, I guess," DC said, remembering the fact himself.

Once Redskin's shirt was off, the chief of the war party let loose a barbaric yell. Snarf jumped. DC's hand went to his gun. But instead of attacking, the Indians lowered their weapons and waded out to meet Redskin. They jabbered cordially, exchanging happy greetings.

"Birds of a feather," DC muttered.

Redskin put his shirt back on and waded toward them, with the war party following behind like so many happy puppies. But his face was hard, like a man who'd been given bad news.

"What's goin on?" DC asked.

"We have been invited to their camp."

"To their camp? Tell em thanks, but no thanks."

"It is not an invitation we may refuse," Redskin said, packing.

They were well and truly surrounded by the war party now. DC faked a smile at the Chief. He did not smile back.

21

The sun never rose that day. The gray dawn revealed a spattering of teepees and cookfires bordering a forest which would have looked welcoming had it not been for the eerily silent and somber-faced women and children watching their arrival. The Chief made an announcement and smiles broke out everywhere. Redskin was mobbed again, this time by the women and children.

Snarf and DC exchanged a look. Neither of them had the foggiest idea what was going on or what Redskin had done to earn his celebrity, but it was obvious to them both that he wasn't enjoying it.

They dismounted outside the Chief's teepee, and the Chief went inside. DC and Snarf made to follow, but Redskin stopped them. "Wait here," he ordered.

DC didn't like an Indian telling him what to do, but these were extenuating circumstances if ever there were any. A gaggle of half-naked Indian children accumulated around them, staring at their white skin and strange clothing.

"What do you think's goin on in there?" Snarf asked.

"I donno, but we'll find out here in a minute if we can trust Redskin."

"What d'you mean?"

"Well, if he was to decide he didn't want to split the gold with us, now would be the time."

"I trust him."

DC snorted, "You trust him. You trust everybody."

Redskin emerged from the teepee. "We cannot leave," he announced. And then he walked away.

"Wait a minute!" DC said, grabbing his arm. "What do you mean we can't leave? You got these people wrapped round your finger. Just tell em you've got to go."

"They will not let us."

"Let us? Did you try..." DC lowered his voice and looked around for eavesdroppers, "...tellin em about the gold? We could cut em in if they-"

"Gold does not interest them."

"We could turn the gold into wampum if-"

"Sheriff, they cannot be bought. Not with anything you can give."

DC's eyes narrowed. "But they want somethin. Somethin from you. And you don't wanna give it."

"I cannot give it," Redskin bit back. Then he softened, but he was reluctant to explain. Finally, he confessed, "They want to fight me."

"Fight you?" DC demanded.

"The coyote is their proving ground. A sacred place of testing for the young men who are ready to become warriors. But, since Matthew Craney came, the coyote has been lost to them. Without it, they cannot add warriors to their ranks."

"What's that got to do with you?"

"Before I was chosen to be a Spiritwalker, I was a Red Chief."

"Red Chief?"

"Many tribes of my people have two chiefs, a white and a red. The white leads in time of peace. The red leads in time of war."

DC tried to digest the idea that the pacifist Indian he'd been sleeping beside and galloping with all buddy-buddy used to be a chief and a war chief to boot. It stuck in his craw. He pointed at the Chief who stood watching their talk flanked by warriors, "What about him? Why can't he do it?"

"No red chief can make warriors from his own tribe."

"'From his own tribe.' Well, I for one would never suspect an Indian of cheatin," DC said sarcastically.

"What happens if you don't fight?" Snarf asked.

"They will kill us at sunset," Redskin admitted.

DC's eyes sharpened. Snarf paled. The camp fell silent. All eyes were on them. "Lemme get this straight," DC whispered. "These redskins wanna fight you, but you won't do it, so they're gonna kill us."

"That is correct."

"Will they fight me? I'm a sheriff. Isn't that kinda like a Red Chief?"

Redskin turned to the Chief and said something to him in Indian. The Chief answered back and everyone in the tribe laughed.

"What'd he say?"

"He said, 'No white-nothing can make a warrior.'"

DC fumed. "White-nothing. So we're gonna die on your scruples?"

"I am accountable only for my actions. Not the actions of others."

"Not the actions of others," DC muttered to himself as he thought it over. "Ok then," he said. Then he hauled back and punched Redskin in the face.

Indian warriors, whooping wildly, leapt on DC, dragged him to the ground, and tied his wrists and ankles.

"No!" Snarf cried.

One raised a huge club, ready to smash in his skull, but the Chief bellowed.

The club froze over DC's head.

All eyes were on the Chief... His finger moved and pointed at Snarf.

Snarf didn't even have time to get scared. Rough red hands seized him, bent his arms painfully behind his back, and forced him to his knees. The club went up again. Snarf squeezed his eyes shut, hoping that when the club smashed in his skull, his eyes wouldn't burst out of their sockets.

A gunshot split the air - Redskin! He stood by DC, who was still tied up, but he held the sheriff's smoking pistol, pointed up at the sky.

Having spent his life in a saloon, Snarf had seen a lot of angry men. He was a sort of anger connoisseur. He'd seen the kind of crazy anger provoked by alcohol, he'd seen the hot anger of a man who'd lost everything in a game of cards, he'd seen the fiery anger of wounded pride, and he'd seen the cold bitter anger of a man who'd lost his wife and baby during the tightrope walk of childbirth. But none of the anger he'd ever seen compared to the anger he saw then in Redskin's eyes. It was bloody, monstrous anger. It was wrath.

Redskin spat out some Indian talk, and Snarf was dragged aside and released. DC, still tied up, was deposited like a sack of potatoes beside him.

The Indians formed a ring with Redskin and the Indian with the club in the middle. The Indian, who wore only a loin-cloth, tossed his club to a friend and readied himself for a fight - feet shoulder width apart, weight on his toes, hands spread and ready. Redskin kept his shirt on, and he stood flat footed, seemingly completely unprepared. But his eyes blazed.

The Chief made a noise.

The Indian dove at Redskin, shrieking like a banshee.

Redskin caught the Indian's oncoming head and brought his knee up into his face. His nose crunched. The Indian went limp as a puppet with cut strings and lay, unmoving, in the grass.

Snarf looked at DC. DC looked at Snarf. It had happened so fast both of they thought they might have imagined it. They hadn't.

Redskin put his hand on the unconscious Indian and made an announcement. The tribe cheered. His family dragged him from the ring.

A second Indian, wiry with muscle, stepped forward and assumed the same ready stance as the first. Redskin remained flat footed. The fire in his eyes wasn't blazing anymore. It was cold and hard. The Chief gave the signal.

Instead of diving at Redskin, the second Indian launched a blinding number of punches and kicks at such speed that the individual attacks could hardly be seen, but none of them touched Redskin, who moved languidly out of the way of each blow.

The Indians cheered the display.

Eventually, there was an opening, and Redskin struck, snapping one of the Indian's ribs like it was a twig. The Indian clamped his arm down over the rib and fought on. He threw a kick at Redskin, but Redskin caught his ankle and lifted it, tossing the Indian onto his back. Redskin's fists came down like pistons, breaking ribs and splitting skin. In half a second, the Indian looked like he'd fallen into a meat grinder.

His shirt spattered with blood, Redskin put a bloody hand on the Indian's chest and made the same announcement as before. The tribe cheered again. The Indian, clutching his liquified ribs and spitting blood, crawled away, beaming.

Before a third challenger could step forward, before the Chief could give the signal, two Indians shot at Redskin like arrows and drove him to the ground. The watching Indians roared - some their approval at the sneaky attack, some their disapproval at the lack of decorum. Either way, there was nothing to be done now; it was two on one.

But to say that Redskin counted as a single man would be a gross misrepresentation of his skills. It would be more accurate to say that this third fight was 2 on 10. Redskin slipped out of every hold they tried to get him into and, while they came at him with feet and fists, he came at them with feet, fists, knees, elbows, head, forearms, and shins. Every part of him was transformed into a weapon of painful precision. At one point, he dug his chin into the spine of one opponent, causing a blood-curdling scream.

The other opponent grabbed Redskin's shirt and tore it off him. The Indian women, who had not seen Redskin shirtless in the river, gasped. Snarf and DC, who had been too far away at the river to see anything more than a silhouette, couldn't believe their eyes. Horrible red scars covered Redskin's torso. They rippled over his ribs in thick weals and streaked down his back. The soft flesh of his middle was unscarred, but more scars started around the hard bone of his hips and disappeared beneath his pants. Redskin looked like he'd crawled through the teeth of some vicious animal.

His wrath became bloodlust. In the blink of an eye, he had one neck clamped in a headlock and the other neck clamped in a leg lock and he was squeezing with all his might. The trapped Indians thrashed like fish, but they could not escape. One of them turned purple. He collapsed first. The other, his eyes about to bulge out of his head, fought on for a few heartbeats, then he too succumbed and lay limp. But Redskin did not let go. Some neck bones popped.

Redskin blinked. His eyes focused on something or someone to his right. All the bloodlust went out of him. Snarf took a breath - his first in a long time, he realized.

The wives of the men who'd been fighting rushed into the

ring and tended their husbands. They were alive, barely, and would tell for many years how they had seen the spirits of their ancestors beckoning. Redskin tried to move away, but the wives pawed at him and begged him for something. Redskin put his hands on his opponents and said the necessary words.

The rest of the Indians swarmed him, whooping and cheering - even the ones with the broken nose and broken ribs cheered as best they could. The Chief raised Redskin's arm in victory and hailed his prowess.

Someone untied DC. He and Snarf watched as Redskin came toward them. His body, hot from the exertion of fighting, smoked in the drizzling rain like a piece of molten iron that had been quenched.

"Tomorrow they will take us to the coyote," Redskin said, pushing past them. He grabbed his bag and headed toward the woods.

Snarf and DC watched him go. The Indians pawed at them, trying to get them to join in the celebration. One of them shoved a bowl of hot food into DC's hands, and he took it, letting them pull him toward the cook fire. But Snarf broke away and ran after Redskin, who was disappearing into the distant forest.

22

Snarf looked up in awe at the cathedral of trees that sprang out of the prairie without warning. The tall white trunks stretched like columns to heaven. And the wind whispered prayers as it wound its way through the supplicating branches.

When Snarf broke away from the feast, he'd planned to shout for Redskin at the border of the forest until the Indian came out. The idea now seemed sacrilegious in the extreme. One did not shout in this place. Snarf took off his hat before he went in.

Redskin's trail was easy to follow because he'd made no attempt to hide it. If he had, a pack of bloodhounds couldn't have found him.

Snarf heard Redskin before he saw him. He couldn't make out the words, distant and muffled by the forest as they were, but he angled toward their source, going as silently as he could. Eventually, he saw the Indian through the trees. He was close enough now to hear his words clearly.

"And when he had given thanks," Redskin said, reading from his big gilded book, "he brake it," Redskin broke a piece of bread, "and said, 'Take, eat: this is my body, which is broken for you: this do in remembrance of Me.'" Redskin ate the bread.

"After the same manner also, he took the cup," Redskin raised a small wooden cup, "when he had supped, saying, 'This cup is the new testament in my blood: this do ye, as oft as ye drink it, in remembrance of Me.'" Redskin drank whatever was in the cup and set it aside. Then he looked up. He had tears on his cheeks.

"It's alive," Redskin said. "Great Father, it's alive in me again. I- I can feel it... clawing."

Snarf shivered because Redskin was blood-earnest, deadly-serious, and obviously terrified of whatever it was that was inside him.

"Help!" Redskin pleaded through gritted teeth. "Help me to kill my flesh. Because..."

Snarf leaned in.

Redskin bowed his head - he couldn't look up because what he was about to say was too shameful- "Oh, Father, I *want*- I *want* it alive. Forgive me; I want it alive." Redskin sobbed. His shoulders heaved. He sank down behind the log so Snarf couldn't see him anymore, but he could still hear him, weeping.

Snarf decided it was time to go.

Then Redskin began wailing.

Once, Unk had shot a dog that they'd caught breaking into The Six at night and eating their stores. His first shot had only wounded it. The dog had flailed, spraying blood, shattering liquor glasses, howling, growling, and yelping until Unk had shot it again and again.

Redskin was like that dog now. Snarf ran, with Redskin's wails echoing through the cathedral of trees.

23

The Indians kept their word. At dawn, a red hand gently pressed Snarf's shoulder, waking him. Outside the teepee, all was fog and mystery. Indian warriors moved about as silently as the undead.

Snarf saddled Mary Beth. He left her girth loose. He didn't care what DC said; cinching it down tight looked uncomfortable.

DC and Boss materialized out of the fog. "Seen Redskin?" DC asked.

Snarf shook his head, not at all eager to confess or describe what he'd seen in the forest yesterday.

DC eyed the warriors gathering around them and grinned. "With these guys with us, Craney don't stand a chance."

Redskin and Beautiful Feet stepped out of the fog. Redskin didn't look at either of them. He kept his eyes on the ground, his normally straight back was hunched. And he did his best to stay away from Snarf.

"About time," DC said. "Let's find ole Chiefy and get outta here."

Redskin caught Snarf staring at him but gave him no greeting. He turned quickly away and mounted Beautiful Feet. Snarf was a little relieved and a little disappointed to be given the cold shoulder. He climbed onto Mary Beth. The saddle slipped a little on account of the loose girth, but he made it up alright.

Soon, all the warriors were assembled. The Chief gave the signal, and they started silently into the fog. When they entered the forest, Snarf couldn't help but glance at Redskin. He sat almost lifeless in his saddle, his eyes fixed on nothing, lost in a fog of his own.

Eventually, the forest thickened. The wide cathedral-spaces filled up with trees, and bracken and the flat ground began to ripple and rise beneath their horses. The river, their constant companion, babbled away off to their left. Sometimes it even peeked and winked at them through the trees.

Redskin rode alone, isolated from the other Indians by the protective bubble of celebrity his mysterious scars had earned him, separated from DC by his renewed status as 'one of them,' and cut off from Snarf for reasons Snarf didn't understand. It made Snarf mad. So he set his cap and rode up to Redskin, but before he could open his mouth, Redskin said, "Stay away."

"Why?" Snarf demanded.

"The Son of the Great Father commands me to cut off even my right hand if it causes me fall off the Way."

"Looks like you got both hands to me."

"You, Snarf, *you* are my right hand."

"Well, I don't wanna be cut off."

Redskin closed his eyes, trying to shut Snarf out.

"What's the matter?"

Redskin kept his eyes closed.

"I saw you in the forest yesterday."

Redskin opened his eyes. They locked on something high up. For a moment, Snarf thought Redskin was going to tell him what was going on, but instead he announced, "We are here."

There was nothing extraordinary about the clearing they'd entered. It was just a clearing like any other, but the distant mountain, visible through the break in the tree canopy, was anything but ordinary.

The mountain was the biggest thing Snarf had ever seen. And the ugliest. Once, maybe, it had been beautiful, but something had marred it, taking huge chunks out of it and leaving behind stony scars where there should have been trees. A few trunks, twisted and wretched, stuck up here and there like dead teeth in the ruined places. It looked like a bone long gnawed by some monstrous wolf.

The mountain's one feature that was still beautiful was the waterfall. Three-quarters of the way up the mountainside, water gushed from some hidden well and fell streaking like white lightning down, down, down through empty space until it crashed, thundering, out of sight.

Snarf slipped the drawing of the coyote out of its case. He looked from it to the mountain. The blood streaming down the coyote's forehead did bear a resemblance to the waterfall...

The Chief started making an announcement. Snarf quickly put the drawing away. A warrior presented DC with a large bundle. "Thanks," DC said with a nod at the Chief, who made another proclamation before he and all the warriors turned and headed back the way they came.

"Hey, wait!" DC shouted. "Where you goin?"

"Kolowissi," the Chief replied. "Kolowissi mountain. No." He made a slashing motion with his hand then he and his warriors disappeared into the woods.

DC looked at Redskin, "Kolowissi?"

"A dragon. They believe he rules this mountain. They will go no further."

"A dragon? Indians believe in dragons?"

"Everyone believes in dragons."

"Not me."

"What's in the package?" Snarf asked.

DC untied the bundle. It turned out to be three military uniforms, the same type worn by Craney's men. DC beamed. "If you can't beat em, join em!" he tossed a uniform to Snarf.

Snarf inspected the tunic. There was a little slit in it, just over the heart and just wide enough for an arrowhead, and there was a red stain around the slit. "I wonder how they got these?" he asked sarcastically.

"Who cares, just put em on."

Snarf dismounted and dressed. He tried to ignore the flashes of Redskin's scarred torso that he saw out of the corner of his eye as the Indian put on his uniform.

"Uh, DC..." Snarf said, turning to display himself to the sheriff. The uniform hung off him everywhere. It was so big it must have belonged to one of Purl's relations.

"What are we gonna do with you?" DC asked, holding up Snarf's dangling sleeve.

24

A uniformed corpse lay limply across Mary Beth's saddle. Had you been fortunate enough to get a close look at the corpse, you would have thought it a strange corpse indeed. Its arms and legs bounced freely and in all directions, as if the bones had been removed or soaked in vinegar. Also, its head was very small. But perhaps it was a deficit of intelligence that caused its demise.

The corpse looked up. It wasn't a corpse at all. It was Snarf disguised as a corpse. The idea had been DC's. A little stuffing and some ropes tying the gloves to Snarf's wrists and the boots to Snarf's ankles pulled off the effect nicely.

"Hold still," DC said.

"But it hurts," Snarf groaned, and the position he lay in was indeed uncomfortable. Mary Beth's saddle dug into his ribs, and he was constantly slipping, so he had to hold on tight. His fingers ached. "Are we there yet?"

"What about it, Redskin? We close?"

Redskin shook his head and urged Beautiful Feet on toward the mountain.

"Looks like we got a ways to go, deputy. Hang in there,"

DC said, leading the donkey after Redskin. Mary Beth followed behind, carrying Snarf who was moaning over his miserable fate.

As they rode on, DC studied Redskin. The Indian had hardly spoken since he'd wrestled his fellow redskins at the powwow or whatever it was. Now he rode like a man depressed, slumped and hunched in the saddle, with his eyes on his horse's ears. He'd perk up every once in a while to get his bearings then would slump down again. DC had enough experience to know when something had shook loose in a man, and something had definitely shook loose inside Redskin. The question was, what was it? And could Humpty Dumpty get himself back together? "You've, uh, you've never told us how this coyote works," he said because sometimes talk helped a man.

"It is a proving ground," Redskin replied, as if that explained everything.

"Proving ground?"

"A place young men go to face tests. If they pass, they are warriors."

"If they fail?"

"They are dead."

That got Snarf's attention. If Unk had been there, he'd have cashed in his chips. High stakes was one thing. Life and death was something else.

"Why a coyote?" DC asked.

"Coyotes are tricksters. Greedy creatures and liars. By entering a coyote and coming out again, warriors proved they were able to defeat their own greed and deception and were therefore ready to take their place as protectors of the tribe."

DC frowned, "How do you enter a coyote?"

"You will see," Redskin said, turning their course toward the river.

DC followed, looking back to make sure Mary Beth did the

same. She did. She was a good horse. He wasn't too much a man to admit when he was wrong, and he had been wrong about that horse. She was at least ok.

A shadow fell on them, and the forest ended. DC looked up. They'd entered the shadow of Craney's mountain. For the first time, DC wondered if there was enough gold to make all this worth it.

"Hey, DC?" Snarf asked, his voice muffled by Mary Beth's flank. "Where are we?"

Boss stumbled.

DC looked around, and what he saw made his blood run cold. The bare earth between the forest and the riverbank was pockmarked by graves. Some'd been filled in and covered, others were open and empty. A totem pole stood at the head of each grave. Some were new, others were ancient, leaning, and rotted, the animals on them mutilated almost out of recognition by time.

"What is this place?" DC asked.

"A graveyard," Redskin answered.

"Graveyard? What for?"

"For those who do not survive the coyote," Redskin answered. "We are close. We must cross the river,"

A man's voice bellowed, "Ho, there!" He was some distance away and he was waving his arms over his head. There were two other men with him. They all wore military uniforms - Craney's men!

"You cain't cross there!" he shouted. "Cross ere!"

"Stuff your oil rag in your hat an let me do the talkin," DC hissed to Redskin as he turned toward the distant men.

Redskin stuffed his black hair into his hat.

"Whooo-ee!" the man exclaimed when they got closer. "You boys near waltzed yer wampums right into eternity. It's too deep there. Ya gotta cross ere."

"Thanks," DC tipped his hat.

"Jus doin my job. I like gettin paid."

DC led them into the river. As Mary Beth and her 'corpse' passed the man, he took off his hat and put it over his heart.

Into the river they all went. Before they were halfway across, the water was up to DC's knees. The donkey hee-hawed in protest but followed.

Snarf, however, was in trouble. The river was tugging at his tied on boots and gloves. He could feel the ropes slipping. And there was nothing he could do to stop them.

Halfway across, the water lapped over DC's saddle, and Boss was the biggest horse of the bunch.

Snarf felt the saddle shift under him. He squeezed it for dear life, but it was too late, and the girth was too loose. In a rush, it slid off Mary Beth, and he plunged into the icy water, his gloves and boots drifting away in all directions.

"Help!" he cried.

Craney's men, watching from the shore, knuckled their eyes to be sure they were seeing what they were seeing: the dead come to life!

"Help! DC!" Snarf shouted, floundering in the too-big uniform.

"It's them!" one of Craney's men shouted. They drew and opened fire.

Redskin was closest, so he and Beautiful Feet surged hard toward Snarf.

DC fired back at Craney's men. They scattered for cover.

Redskin stretched nearly out of the saddle reaching for Snarf, desperate to clamp his hand on the boy and get him out of the suffocating water, away from the ripping bullets. Snarf, floundering and about to go under, just managed to grab Redskin's hand. The Indian lifted him out of the water as if he weighed nothing. Snarf wrapped his dripping arms around the Indian and squeezed him tight.

DC was on the shore, blasting away at Craney's men. "C'mon!" he urged them.

Beautiful Feet climbed out of the water, soaking and winded. Mary Beth, saddle-less and frustrated, followed. They all dove into the forest with bullets whizzing past their ears.

Snarf clung to Redskin. The Indian's spine bounced against his cheek as they raced through the woods. Mary Beth galloped up beside them, her big eyes full of concern. Snarf tried to tell her with a look that he was ok, but he didn't think she understood. Ahead of them, DC swore at the wretched donkey who saw no reason at all for their hurry.

"Redskin," DC shouted, "is the coyote close? Can we shelter there?"

"No," Redskin shouted back.

A bullet zipped past Snarf's ear. He looked back. Craney's three men from the river had found their horses. The leader had made it across, but the others were still swimming. The outlaw took careful aim on account of the distance and cracked off another shot. It went wide. Thankfully.

Then Beautiful Feet cut hard to the left. Snarf held on tight.

"Down here!" DC cried.

And before Snarf knew it, they were running down a steep hill into a depression. The ground was black, and the depression was an almost perfect circle. It was a dead place, plantless and stony.

When they reached the bottom, almost before they'd come to a stop, DC yanked Snarf off the back of Beautiful Feet and hauled him on foot back up to the top. "Looks like it's time for shootin, deputy," he said as he pushed Snarf down under the cover of the depression's rim.

Snarf fumbled Pap's Pistol off his belt; the too-long, soaking-wet sleeves of the uniform didn't make it easy. "What is this place?" he asked.

"A crater. I bet Craney's been blastin the mountain with dynamite tryin to find his gold."

Suddenly, the huge missing chunks, stony scars, and twisted tree trunks of the ugly mountain took on a new meaning. They were the desperate work of dynamite. What kind of man had the will, and the power, to ruin an entire mountain?

"They're gonna come from there," DC said, pointing at the trees they'd ridden out of. "Stay hidden until they pass. Once their backs're to us, we blast em when I say. Got it?"

"Got it," Snarf said, gripping Pap's Pistol with both hands on account of his sweaty palms. He feared it might squirt out like a piece of soap.

Craney's men came out of the trees just where DC said they would.

Snarf tensed. DC stayed loose. "Not yet..." he whispered.

The trio slowed, looking around for signs of their quarry. But, seeing nothing, they rode past.

"You take the one on the right. I'll take the other two."

Snarf took aim. The six enormous barrels of Pap's Pistol made it seem like he was pointing a cannon at the back of the distant man.

"When I say..."

Snarf licked his lips. His pepperbox hovered over his target
- *target!* - it was a person! He went cold all over.

"Now!"

DC's gun boomed twice. The leader fell. His horse ran off. The man on the left turned in his saddle to see where the shots had come from. He was unhurt. DC fired twice more. His first went wide. His second took the man in the meat of his leg. The man clamped a hand down on the wound and drew a bead on DC. They fired at the same time, but the sheriff's aim was truer. The man dropped dead. His horse stood there wondering what had happened.

But the man on the right, the one Snarf was supposed to shoot, was charging at them. He had the reins in his teeth and a pistol in each hand.

"Deputy!" DC had time to yell, but Snarf was frozen. He hadn't fired a single shot, and DC only had a single shot left.

Bullets chipped at the depression's rim.

"Shoot him!" DC cried.

But the man was close now. He was bigger than the barrel of Snarf's gun and riding at him like a demon.

DC stood up. The oncoming outlaw opened up on him with both barrels, but DC had presented his flank, a slim target. He raised his pistol and fired.

The blast blew all the noise out of the world and slowed the very wheels of time.

The seed of DC's bullet blossomed, and red meat burst from the horse's breast. Its metronome, its heart, exploded. Its front hooves came down out of rhythm. It fell, launching the gun-toting outlaw right at the sheriff.

But DC just stepped aside, like a man changing partners at a dance, and the outlaw sailed past. The black ground dropped away under the sailing outlaw and then reached up and smashed him into eternity.

DC stood on the rim above Snarf like a colossus. The rising sun flamed on his badge and caught the smoking copper casings as they fell from his pistol's hot cylinder. DC's strong fingers worked fresh bullets into the chambers. Snarf heard the cylinder snap home, and the wheels of time caught and flew on again.

DC looked down at him - looked down at him in every sense of the phrase - but only for a moment. Then he remembered Snarf was just a kid. "You'll come through next time, deputy," he said.

The broken outlaw lay at the bottom of the depression. Redskin knelt over him, feeling for any life still pounding in him, but there was none. The broken outlaw's dead horse lay just an arm's length away from Snarf. He could see himself in its glassy eyes. A ways off, the horse that had lost his master had found him again, but he was dead, as was the third outlaw who lay facedown in a patch of stringy grass.

One man. One man with guts had done it all. In less than half a minute and with just six bullets, he'd brought death to three men and a horse. The weight of the act bore down on Snarf. It was like Billy had said: it couldn't be undone. A man could pull a trigger in a second, but what happened after went on forever. Snarf thought of the gutshot man doubled-over in The Six. He'd done that.

All of a sudden Pap's Pistol felt impossibly heavy. DC said he'd knew Snarf would come through the next time, but Snarf wasn't sure he wanted there to be a next time. The kind of power packed into Pap's Pistol - any pistol - he'd felt it and he didn't want it. Not anymore. And he felt foolish for ever wanting it.

Redskin's eyes were on him. Looking at the Indian, Snarf realized he had another kind of power: the power to stop. All he had to do was announce he didn't want to go on, and it would be over. He could go back to Amity, rebuild The Six. Snarf opened his mouth-

A bugle sounded. High up and clear its call came, echoing from the pinnacle of the mutilated mountain.

"Craney," DC said bitterly.

Snarf shut his mouth. He didn't have the power to stop this any more than he had the power to cast Craney's mountain into the sea. The train had left the station. Snarf hoped it wouldn't go off the rails. DC pulled him to his feet and dragged him toward the horses.

26

Snarf was again clinging to Redskin while Beautiful Feet galloped under them. They'd abandoned all attempts at stealth. Now it was a race to the Coyote. The dead trunks of blasted trees whooshed past and the black, rocky ground rushed beneath. Ahead lay a pile of rock. Blasted away from some place higher up, it had fallen in a heap and lay like a collapsed tower of giant's blocks.

The bugle sounded again, this time from behind.

Snarf looked back, and what he saw took his breath away. At least 100 men, all on horseback, all uniformed more-or-less, and all charging at them. Craney didn't have a gang - he had a cavalry!

As Snarf was looking backward, he felt Redskin bend, pressing himself against Beautiful Feet's neck. He turned back around to see what the matter was and found himself staring at an oncoming wall of rock. He had just enough time to throw up his hands.

His elbows took the brunt of the shock. His back bent painfully. One of Beautiful Feet's hooves crashed into his back-side. Then the back of his head hit the ground and everything went black for a split second. Then his vision exploded. Every color of the rainbow danced before his eyes.

He rolled over, coughing and gasping at the same time, trying to get his wind.

"Sheriff!" he heard Redskin shout. "Sheriff, stop!" Redskin had pulled up little more than a stone's throw away. Mary Beth was rearing and stamping. She wanted to run to him, but Redskin held her reins.

"Get to the rocks, deputy!" DC shouted. Then he raised his pistol and fired at Snarf. No! He was firing at Craney's men, who were advancing on Snarf from behind. "The rocks!" DC hollered, turning Boss away.

There was a crevice in the rock pile big enough for Snarf. He scrambled to his feet and ran for the narrow cleft. *Please don't let there be any snakes!* he prayed as he pressed himself into the rocks.

DC and Redskin galloped away hard and reached the forest. DC looked back to check their pursuers, but he didn't see them. Had they lost them? He doubted it. There were too many of them to lose. He pulled Boss to a stop. "Why aren't they following us?" he asked.

Redskin did not know. The woods were stunningly silent after all the gunshots and hoof pounding.

"I don't like it," DC said.

Mary Beth fidgeted against her reins. She wanted to go back for Snarf. Redskin agreed that whatever the silence foreboded, it could not be good for Snarf. "We should go back."

"Go back? Not yet," DC replied, studying the forest with narrowed eyes. "Not yet."

Snarf had wedged himself deep into the rocks, tight as a chuckwalla. He could barely breathe. Except for his pounding heart and heaving breath, all was silent around him. Then something very strange began to happen: the walls of the crevice he'd jammed himself into began to close in on him.

"No!" he hissed through clenched teeth. He pressed against the rock, but it was useless. He was going to be trapped! He knew it was an illusion, like what had happened in the train car, but he couldn't help it. He went slowly, deliberately, in an attempt to keep the fear at bay. But the walls kept closing.

His breathing came in short, ragged gasps. Sweat soaked his shirt despite the cool rock pressing against him. He had to get out, and he had to get out now!

Something landed on the rock above him. He froze. It was hissing. Shaking, he lifted himself up on tiptoes and peeked. A little cylinder, wrapped in red paper like a Christmas present, lay on the rock. A piece of string curled out of one end of it. The far end of the string was burning, and the burning was what made the hissing sound.

It was a stick of dynamite!

Snarf screamed and scrambled toward the exit, banging his knees and elbows in his panic.

"We should go back," Redskin said again to DC.

"Yeah," DC nodded. "Yeah, I think you're right." He turned Boss around and - BOOM! The air jumped. The trees shook. Leaves rained like confetti. A plume of black smoke shot high into the air. The horses reared and screamed, and the donkey fought against his rope.

"What was that?!" DC yelled, hauling on Boss's reins to keep him from bolting.

"Kolowissi," Redskin whispered.

"Dragons ain't real!"

"Dynamite," Redskin clarified. "It was dynamite," he said.

DC looked up at the black smoke rising into the sky above them, blotting out the sun. "You don't think-" he broke off. He couldn't say it. Snarf was dead. Blown to bits. Guilt filled him. He'd brought the kid on this wild goose chase, after all, and loaded his head with dreams of gold and glory, and for what?

"He was my right hand," Redskin whispered, "but I could not cut him off." He looked to his right, his eyes filled with despair, "So you did."

DC hardened his heart against his guilt. "Ain't no goin back," he said, rising high in the saddle and gripping the reins with white knuckles. "Time to get that gold and shove it down Craney's throat."

Redskin had his eyes shut. "Forgive me," he whispered.

"You don't need forgiveness, you need revenge. C'mon," DC cried, urging them into the forest. "Yah!" He drove them away from the rising plume of black smoke and toward unholy vengeance on the man who'd made it.

27

Everything sounded fuzzy to Snarf, as if he had water in his ears. He was fairly certain dead people could hear; after all, it was important not to speak ill of them, so they must be able to hear something. But he was absolutely sure that dead people did not breathe. So, because he could hear the rasping sound of his breath going slowly in and out, he thought he was alive. At least, a little bit alive.

Something cold and wet pawed at his cheek. It was rough, like a cat's tongue. It started on his right cheek, licking away at the place where his jaw hinged. Then it moved up over his temple and onto his forehead.

He pried open his eyes.

He was in a dim room. The walls were papered: yellow with thin blue stripes, like the pinstripes on a man's trousers. The ceiling was whitewashed and very clean. He was lying in a feather bed. The covers were as puffy as a cloud and just as soft. He'd never lain in such a bed in all his life.

The cold rough wet thing withdrew from his cheek. As it went away, he saw that it was a washcloth held in a feminine hand. The arm the hand belonged to was bare and strong with that supple kind of strength reserved only for the fairer sex. Just before the bend in the elbow, there was a bunch of fabric where the sleeves had been rolled up. He followed the arm until it connected to the shoulder and he followed the shoulder until it became the neck. The neck was long, elegant, and pale, like a Roman column. Atop the neck, of course, was the head, and the head, naturally, contained the face. It was a naturally beautiful face, unpainted but rosy cheeked and red lipped. She wasn't more than 14. Her dark, golden hair, held back from her face with a bandana, fell in gentle curls to her shoulders. She made no movement to acknowledge that he was awake. Her eyes did not meet his. She washed his face as if it were nothing more than a dirty spot on a floor.

From the other side of the bed, a woman said, "Hello."

Snarf turned. It was Jewel. She sat at his bedside in a wing-backed chair, with her gloved fingers laced over the top of her cane. His mouth was suddenly very dry.

She smiled at him, "How are you feeling?" her voice was soft and motherly.

"Ok," he rasped.

"You've had quite the experience," she said while the other woman dabbed away at his forehead with her washcloth.

"How did you- I thought the train-" his addled brains couldn't form the question he wanted to ask.

"How did I get here so fast? Some soldiers lent me the use of their horses. Fine animals. Sadly, they did not survive."

"The soldiers or the horses?"

Jewel smiled like a sphinx.

Snarf swallowed.

The washcloth withdrew from his forehead. "There," Jewel said, looking him over, "good as new." That was a lie. His face was clean, but his neck was filthy, and his ear was caked with dirt and blood. Jewel rose smoothly and headed for the door.

"Come, Eden," she ordered and the girl, Eden, Snarf assumed, followed with the washcloth and basin.

As Jewel opened the door to leave, Snarf saw a man in the dark hallway. He was smoking a cigarette. Jewel stepped close to him as Eden passed behind her and he thought Jewel spoke to him for a moment, but he couldn't hear what she said. Then Jewel disappeared downstairs.

The man took a drag on his cigarette and looked at Snarf through the cracked door. Snarf thought he detected malice in the glance, but before he could be sure, the man tossed his cigarette to the floor and stamped it out. Then he came into the room.

Somehow, in person, Matthew Craney looked so much bigger than he had in the photograph, and his size wasn't just due to the fact that Snarf was lying prone in a feather bed either. Matthew Craney was tall - more than six feet tall - and broad. He was a big, big man with the bad knees to prove it. He had sticks of red dynamite stuffed in his belt. These he slid to his hip so he could sit in the wing-back chair Jewel had occupied a moment ago. "Hi, son," he said.

Snarf didn't say a word. He was frozen like a mouse before a cobra.

"Ease up a bit there. You look like someone's walked over your grave."

"You're Matthew Craney," he managed to say.

"Sure am," Craney mumbled around the cigarette he was lighting. "And you're in my bed," he said after he'd blown out the smoke.

Snarf moved to push the covers down, but Craney stopped him. "No, no, no. Hospitality's a lost art. I insist." Craney pulled the covers back up and tucked them under Snarf's chin, rather too tightly, Snarf thought. "If I had some questions," Craney went on, "do you think you could rustle up some answers?"

Snarf nodded.

"We'll start with an easy one: what's your name?"

"Snarf."

"That's a good name…" Craney took a drag on his cigarette, "for a pirate."

Snarf had heard no question, so he said nothing.

Craney squinted at him, "And that's what you are, aren't you? A pirate. Going after buried treasure and scallawags."

It is impossible to overstate the weakness of Snarf's position. He did not know where he was in the world except that he was lying in a feather bed, with his arms trapped under the covers and the covers pulled up to his chin. He was, from Craney's perspective, just a disembodied head. That gave him an idea. He felt for Pap's Pistol.

Craney smiled. "It's alright. I'm a pirate too." He held up Snarf's gunbelt, with Pap's Pistol dangling from it."I hear this thing fires off all six at once. That true?"

Snarf nodded, "But I cleaned it, so it should do one at a time now."

"That's good. Next question: where are you from?"

"Amity," Snarf answered.

"Amity," Craney beamed, "Amity means friendship. We're friends, aren't we?" He asked before taking a long drag on his cigarette. Snarf watched the end of it burn like hellfire, then he nodded. Sure, they were friends.

"Good. Speaking of friends, I sent one of my friends to meet you at the train station. What happened to him?"

Snarf remembered the rat-faced man with the round hat and the silver knife. "He missed the train," he answered, feeling some of his old impetuosity.

"He did?" Craney shook his head as if he couldn't believe the bad luck. "That's a shame." He ruminated on the misfortune for a moment then decided there was nothing that could be done. "Well, tell me, friend," he reached for something in his back pocket, "where is this coyote?" He held up the drawing.

Snarf suddenly felt very cold. He had no idea where the coyote was. None at all. And both Craney and the coyote had the same hungry look in their eyes.

Craney waited, motionless as a hawk, but Snarf was too scared to confess his ignorance.

"Listen, son, I've blown away half this mountain looking for the gold. So, if you tell me where it's hidden, do you think I'm going to be mad?"

"I- I don't know," Snarf said huskily.

Craney cocked his ear, "Say again?"

"I said, I don't know where the coyote is," Snarf repeated.

Craney's hand shot out like a viper, seized Snarf by the collar, and hauled him out of bed. Snarf cried out, but Craney ignored him and hauled him into the hallway and down the stairs.

28

The screen door banged open when Craney slammed into it. He dragged Snarf out of the house and onto a porch complete with rocking chairs and a checkerboard on a barrel. Snarf's bare feet scrambled under him, but he couldn't gain his footing because Craney was moving too fast and holding him too low to the ground. His grip was like iron. Then they were off the porch and on the street. Craney's house, a huge plantation style mansion, white and massive and awesome in the middle of the virgin forest, loomed over them. The damp air felt pressurized, like the air inside a drum when it's struck, and the fuzziness Snarf had heard in the house was now a ceaseless roar.

Then Snarf realized he was being dragged down a street- a real dirt street, not some forest path, and there were other houses besides Craney's and other buildings too. Indeed, there was a whole town, and people to go with it. Men, women, children, and animals followed them down the thoroughfare.

All the men, and there must have been hundreds of them, wore military uniforms, but the uniforms had been customized with paint or jewelry. Tattoos laced their arms. Their hair shone with bear grease, and they bristled with guns. The women wore dresses, cut plain and simple, like the one Eden had worn. The children were naked or clothed in rags like cannibals.

Snarf had no words for the fear gripping him then. They'd set out expecting a gang of five or six, but here was an entire town's worth of outlaws, and they all had families – wives and children and everything!

He craned his neck toward the source of the ceaseless roaring and saw the waterfall. They were about 200 feet below its crest, so the water was white and foaming as it streamed endlessly past like salt pouring from a can. An outcropping hung over the empty space in front of the waterfall. On the outcropping was a gallows. A man stood by with a noose in his hand.

Craney shoved Snarf into the man's arms. He felt the noose go over his neck and he felt the man cinch it down tight. Snarf looked at him and wished he hadn't. It was Flint!

"Since you're a pirate," Craney yelled over the roar of the falls, "I don't think I need to explain your situation to you, but just in case: answer the questions or swing."

Snarf looked down, over the edge of the outcropping. He could see the river far, far below, veiled by a mist of falling water.

"Don't worry," Craney went on, "you're light enough that your neck'll hold. And, if you'll notice, we haven't tied your hands. We like to leave the hands free so you've got a fighting chance. We had one fellow, Three-Day Pete we call him, he managed to get a whole arm through the noose. He lasted three days and his arm turned black before he died."

Snarf shuddered at the idea, and at the cold mist covering him like fever-sweat.

"So tell me, where's the gold?"

"I don't know," Snarf replied desperately.

Craney pushed Snarf back toward the edge of the outcropping. Snarf wrapped his hands around the big man's thick wrist - his hand was clamped on Snarf's collar. Snarf's bare heels tasted empty space. "I don't know where your gold is!" he shouted.

Craney pushed him back just a little more, and one whole foot went off the edge. Snarf twisted crazily, anchored only by his toe, clinging desperately to the outcropping, and Craney's fist gripping the cloth of his collar.

"I don't know - that's what we needed Redskin for! To lead us to the gold! He knows where the coyote is! If you find him, he can show you where it is!"

Craney studied Snarf, trying to decide if he was telling the truth. Eventually he decided the boy was too scared to lie. He pulled Snarf back onto the outcropping and let go of him. Flint took off the noose.

Snarf gulped air as Craney walked toward the townspeople who'd gathered to watch. He made some announcement Snarf couldn't hear. The men dispersed, as if they'd been ordered out on a mission. Craney came back. "You're having dinner with us," he announced.

Snarf hung his head. He was a stool-pigeon, a traitor, and covered in shame.

Flint shoved him, so he followed Craney through the tunnel made for him by the townspeople. Snarf's soaked skin crawled to feel so many eyes on him. But none of them spoke. That was the weirdest part; no one said a word.

Jewel was on the porch, smiling at Snarf as he tromped up the steps. "Glad you could join us," she said.

29

The forest grew right up to the sheer wall of white limestone, making the wall felt rather like an intruder whose presence was resented. The wall wasn't entirely unjustified in its feelings, for trees have a long memory, and they remembered the time, eons ago, when the wall had thrust itself rudely out of the ground, sundering their roots and dividing their families. They wanted nothing more than for the impertinent wall to sink back down from wherever it had come. They did not care that such a feat was beyond the wall's powers, that it had been thrust up against its own will and at great pain to its person. They wanted it gone. They were a spoiled, self-righteous bunch of trees, used to getting their own way no matter how long it took.

The Indian and the Sheriff, sneaking their way through the tangled trunks, were oblivious to the conflict between the trees and the wall because each was embroiled in a conflict of his own: Redskin with his despair, DC with his guilt.

A particularly nasty bunch of trees appeared. In their midst stood a blasted willow, black and burned by lightning. No living thing knew what sin the willow committed that caused such wrath to come down upon it. Perhaps it committed no sin. Perhaps, like the blind man in John's Gospel, it had been blasted to make a totem, a sign of holy wrath to all who looked upon it.

Redskin dismounted beside the nasty bunch of trees. He stuck his head between their tangled trunks then pulled it out again a moment later. "This is it," he announced. Taking Beautiful Feet's reins, he led her into the trees. DC dismounted Boss and followed.

The trees shielded a crack in the limestone wall. The crack was an inverted V, wide at the bottom, steadily narrowing toward the top until it disappeared altogether. But it wasn't very wide at the bottom, just wide enough for a horse. If a man tried to ride his horse through the crack, he'd have found his ankles quite scraped before he penetrated 10 feet.

DC waited for Redskin, Beautiful Feet, and Mary Beth to get a ways into the crack before he followed with Boss and the donkey; he had no desire to get kicked in the face by a nervous mare.

The crack smelled like stale chalk powder and ran more-or-less straight into the rock wall. After a while, it became very dark. Then DC felt air on his face, and suddenly the walls of the crack disappeared. They had entered a large open place, a sort of cave or atrium. He couldn't see how big it was because of the darkness, but he could sense its vastness in the sudden change of sound.

Redskin sparked a piece of flint and lit a torch. For a moment, DC wondered where he'd gotten the torch, then he saw that the walls were lined with them. Redskin held up his lit torch, and its light filled the space. They seemed to have entered a theater. There were benches carved in the limestone, stair-stepping down to a stage. Some kind of figure was on the stage. A big thing, shadowy and dark.

"What is this place?" DC asked.

"The coyote," Redskin answered before descending toward the stage. Beautiful Feet and Mary Beth followed, cautious on account of the unfamiliar steps.

As they neared the stage, the dancing torchlight illuminated the shadowy figure. It was a coyote's head, hewn out of the stone and as huge as four wagons stacked two on two. Its mouth was open, and its lips were drawn back, revealing ghostly white teeth. The flickering firelight of their torches seemed to make its red tongue dance. The stone that formed the coyote's head was black. The still-visible chisel marks of its long dead craftsmen gave the impression of thickly matted hair. They'd painted a red stripe between its eyes, around its muzzle, and down its chin to the stage, which was solid red, a field of blood. A dead man dangled half in, half out of the coyote's mouth. A gun lay on the stage by his rotted hand. Billy's spooky drawing hadn't done the coyote justice. Not by a long shot.

DC looked at the gun by the dead man's hand, then up at the little slit of light at the top of the steps they'd just descended. "This must be the barve who shot Billy in the back."

Redskin put his torch into the coyote's mouth, making it look like it was breathing fire. "It is a door."

DC bent but saw only empty darkness down the coyote's throat. "A door. A door to what?"

"The boys who entered the coyote's mouth did not know what tests they would face. Neither do we."

"It stinks," DC said. And the air from the coyote's mouth did indeed stink. But, if he had to go through a little stink to get Craney's gold, that was ok. He yanked the corpse out of the coyote's mouth and took the torch from Redskin. He wasn't about to let the Indian set the seat of his pants on fire. He climbed into the coyote's mouth.

30

The air in the coyote's throat reeked. If it hadn't been for the torch smoking in his face as he crouch-walked down the throat, DC probably wouldn't have made it. Finally, he slid down the back of the throat and into a cave. His boots landed on rock. He took a breath of the rancid air and had to fight down bile. Redskin stood beside him.

DC raised the torch high over his head. It illuminated the boots of the other five men Billy had killed. Black blood covered the backs of their uniforms. The corpses bent awkwardly up at the waist, like men who'd died pounding against a wall and, indeed, they had died against a wall. A wall of gold.

Brick after brick of solid gold stood in a wall 10 feet high. How thick it was, DC couldn't tell because it stretched as far to the left and as far to the right as he could see. The torch made the gold glitter, and the glittering gold quenched the guilt that had been filling him.

There was more gold here than he'd imagined in his wildest dreams. A man could do anything, anything at all, with the wealth in this cave. He could buy himself a whole state if he wanted!

Redskin announced, "I am going now."

"What?!"

The Indian was turning to climb back into the coyote's throat. DC blocked him. "Hey, hey, hey, you can't leave."

"Why not? You have your gold."

"I may have the gold, but I need your help to load it and, besides, don't you want half?"

"I was offered only one-hundred dollars."

"A hundred dollars. Snarf's dead. You can have his share if you stay and help."

Redskin didn't want a single ounce of the gold.

"This is the only way to make Craney pay." DC said, "Make him howl."

"I do not want to make Craney howl." Redskin made again to climb back into the coyote.

DC blocked him with the torch. "Sorry, but... what if he catches you? You might... tell him where the gold is, and... if I'm still here..."

"I will not betray you," Redskin said, pushing to leave.

DC drew his pistol. "I'm sorry," he said, his badge glittering in the torchlight.

Redskin looked at the pistol pointed at him. Then he looked to his right at the person he imagined was always there.

DC's palm sweated against his pistol's grip. He remembered what Redskin had done to those Indians in the village.

But Redskin just looked at him and asked, "What would you have me do?"

31

Snarf stared at his empty plate. He could feel Craney studying him, but he didn't care. The place setting was nice. White china, an array of silverware that was real silver, unlike the cheap tin stuff they'd had at The Six, and a thick white napkin. But Snarf didn't care. He was worried about the soldiers combing the woods at that very moment, looking for the friends he'd betrayed.

Craney's eyes flicked to Jewel then back to Snarf. "You like steak?" he asked.

Snarf didn't speak or move. Craney noticed his ear was caked with dirt and blood. "Your ears ringing?" he asked as he snapped his finger near Snarf's ear.

Snarf shied away.

"Good. That means your drums held. If they weren't ringing, you'd be in trouble. You wouldn't be the first man to lose his ears to dynamite."

A woman, not Eden, but dressed identically and with a face just as beautiful, came in with a plate of steaks. She put one on Craney's plate.

"Guests first," Jewel said, her eyes flashing at the obvious mistake.

The woman, pale now, moved the steak quickly to Snarf's plate. It dripped on the tablecloth. Jewel closed her eyes and breathed out through her nose.

The woman went white as a ghost, "I'm sorr-"

"Do not speak!"

Stifling a whimper, she got a steak onto Craney's plate, then Jewel's. Then she vanished into the kitchen. Another woman, dressed and beautiful like the others, set a bowl of mashed potatoes and gravy on the table. She too withdrew, and they were alone again.

"Potatoes, dear?" Jewel asked Snarf with a smile. But Snarf was watching the blood oozing from his steak, streaking toward him like the arm of an octopus.

Craney gave Jewel a nod, so she plopped some of the mashed potatoes onto Snarf's plate. They'd been red potatoes, and they'd been mashed with the skin on. She put a scoop on Craney's plate, and he dug in before she'd served herself.

"How is it, dear?" Jewel asked.

"Fine." Craney looked at Snarf and saw he wasn't eating. "What do you think?" he asked.

Snarf was still staring at his plate. The blood had surrounded the white potatoes.

"What's the matter, son?" Craney asked.

Snarf didn't know where to begin.

"Are you scared?"

Snarf shook his head and started to cry. "I betrayed him. And DC. And now you're gonna kill em," he sobbed.

Craney snorted, "Kill? Who said anything about killing?"

"Your soldiers. Didn't you send em out..." Snarf trailed off.

"No!" Craney cried, an expression of pain on his face. "I didn't send them out to kill anybody."

"Then-"

"I sent them out with a message."

"A message?"

"Sure," Craney nodded reassuringly, and he took Snarf's hand.

"What message?"

"You really want to know?"

Snarf nodded and wiped away his tears.

Craney tipped his head back, took his hand from Snarf's and put it to his mouth, to amplify the sound. He hollered over the huge dining room table, "Bring the Indian or the gold to the top of the waterfall before midnight," he paused dramatically with a wry smile on his lips and a sly look out of the corner of his eye at Snarf, "or the boy hangs!"

Snarf felt something inside him drop, like what happens when you look down from a tall place, and he suddenly felt very small, like the table was too high and the silverware too big - it was if he'd shrunk down to a baby's size.

"Why the long face?" Craney asked.

Jewel hid a smile by wiping her mouth, which had yet to taste a morsel.

"You don't think they'll come?" Craney prodded.

Snarf snarfed.

Craney patted Snarf's hand gently, as if he were a doctor comforting a terminally ill patient. "Have faith. They'll come."

"You think so?"

"I've seen this lots of times. They always come."

Encouraged, Snarf snarfed again and took up his silverware.

Jewel's lips were pursed to keep from laughing. Craney winked at her. Her eyes sparkled.

Oblivious to the little moment being shared by his hosts, Snarf took a bite of bloody steak. It really was very good, almost as good as the steaks he'd been famous for a lifetime ago in Amity. But had he known it was his last meal, he might have asked if there were any biscuits and honey to go with it.

32

DC kept his gun trained on Redskin with one hand while he loaded bars of gold into Boss's saddle bag with the other. Redskin held the torch and watched. The torch was heavy, like a club. Except it was better than a club because it was on fire. Anything hit with it would not survive the first blow. He tried to banish the thought. He succeeded. Mostly.

DC straightened and stretched his back.

"Are you sure you do not want my help?" Redskin asked.

DC was sure. The idea of the Indian touching his gold galled him because he could see now that Redskin didn't give two bits about the kid and never had. If he did, he'd want to cram it down Craney's throat just as bad as he did, but the Indian just wanted to leave like a whipped dog. Why Redskin had come along, DC couldn't fathom; proselytes for his cocka-mamy religion probably. Grunting, he hoisted the saddle bag onto his shoulder. "Gimme the torch," he commanded.

Redskin obeyed and breathed a sigh of relief that DC hadn't noticed that he'd had to give just the slightest tug to get the torch out of his hand.

DC now had the torch in one hand, his gun in the other,

and the heavy bag of gold over his shoulder. He motioned for Redskin to enter the coyote's throat.

"Let me carry it," Redskin said, reaching for the bag's strap.

DC raised his gun. "No thanks," he said, his eyes hard.

Redskin crawled into the throat. DC followed, grunting with the weight of the gold and keeping his gun trained on Redskin's back.

After they crawled out of the mouth, DC put the gold on Boss. It was not the first bag, nor would it be the last.

Accustomed to the routine, Redskin had his hand out for the torch. DC shook his head - he'd noticed the little tug on the torch after all - and waved with his gun for Redskin to go back into the coyote. Redskin obliged.

DC cast a wary eye over the empty amphitheater. It would be easy for a thief to hide in that darkness and snatch a gold bar from one of the saddle bags. But he had no choice - not if he wanted all of it, and he desperately wanted all of it. If Craney didn't pay to the last penny, then he didn't pay.

33

"Most men, when they hear about me, think it's just me and a few desperate desperados holed up in a mountain cave somewhere wondering who we're gonna eat first," Craney joked as he walked down the main street of his little town with one arm around Jewel's waist and other over Snarf's shoulders. Jewel laughed. They were like a little family on an after-dinner walk.

Thankfully, they were not walking toward the gallows.

"There's been more than one bounty hunter who's showed up looking to cash in on me and instead decided to join up," Craney continued, waving at a blacksmith as they passed. The blacksmith waved back and seemed to glow brighter than his forge after being acknowledged by the Great Man himself. "Any guesses as to why?"

Snarf realized Craney's question was directed at him. "Why what?" he asked.

"Why men join up instead of trying to take me."

Snarf didn't have a clue.

"It's because I pay well. Or, I did until Billy made his move, but we're putting that to rights right now, aren't we?" He pulled Snarf close playfully, as if it was all a big game, but Snarf was almost in a headlock. He pretended to smile, afraid of what might happen to him if he didn't.

"Come on, I want to show you my new office," Craney said, guiding them toward the building at the end of the street. It bookended one end of the town; the gallows bookended the other. The building was new, so new it had no sign on it yet. The men who were whitewashing it stood aside for them.

Just outside the door, Jewel said, "I think I'll walk on."

Snarf somehow got the uneasy feeling that her leaving them had been prearranged.

Craney kissed her on the cheek, and she left. Then he opened the door. Inside, the building smelled of fresh cut pine and new paper. The floor was brilliantly polished; Unk would have tried to swim in its thick lacquer.

"What is it, do you think?" Craney asked.

At first, Snarf thought it was a jail on account of the iron bars, but then he noticed the open vault. "It's a bank," he said.

"Exactly," Craney replied, pleased that Snarf was able to guess so quickly. That was the sign of good architecture. "And this is my office," he gestured toward an open door.

Snarf looked into it. The office had no windows. It was very dark. "It's nice," he lied.

"Go on in," Craney said.

Reluctantly, Snarf went into the office and pretended to look around. Craney hung in the doorway like a spider, watching him eagerly, as if he were waiting for him to make a discovery.

There was a desk, a chair, a calendar, ink pens, some paper, and a photograph.

Craney's eyes glinted.

It was a silver halide print in a golden frame and it showed Jewel and Craney standing in a living room very much like the one Snarf had just been in. There was a young man between them; he was maybe six or seven. The only remarkable thing about him was that there was nothing at all remarkable about him. He was just an ordinary kid. Jewel held his hand, and Craney's big paw rested heavily on his shoulder.

"That's my son," Craney said, his chest swollen with pride.

Snarf wanted to be sick. The idea of having Craney and Jewel for parents made knots in his stomach. And for the first time in his life, he was glad that his parents had left no impression on his memory because impressions, he now realized, could be dangerous.

"Don't worry," Craney said, "he's not here."

"I'd run away too," Snarf said. Fear shot through him as the bold words left his big mouth.

But Craney laughed. "He didn't run away," he picked up the photo and looked at his son. His eyes were loving, but there was also hurt in them. "No, he didn't run away," he said again, this time it seemed to himself. "We sent him away. I just... couldn't give him what he needed. But I will." Craney smiled at Snarf, and the hurt vanished or was banished from his eyes. He put the photo back on the desk and guided Snarf out of the office.

As they stepped out of the bank, Snarf had a view of the whole town. Buildings lined the street, and people walked to and fro, but there was something false about it. Something hollow. If Snarf had been of Easter's frame of mind, he might have thought the hollow feeling was because the town had no church. But that was just a symptom - remember the Kremlin is positively riddled with churches. No, the only clue Snarf could see was the gallows silhouetted by the cascading waterfall.

Craney breathed in deeply, like God must have at the end of the sixth day when he surveyed all he'd made. "In a way, that's what this place is all about." Craney said. "It's a gift. A gift for my son." He looked down at Snarf, but this time Snarf kept his mouth shut.

Craney crouched, wincing on account of his bad knees, so they were eye to eye with only the distant gallows dangling between them. "Did you know we, these generous United States, built schools for the Indians?" Craney asked.

Snarf didn't know that. And he had no idea what it had to do with anything.

"We did. The idea was to reform the savages. Whiten em up a bit. 'Kill the Indian, save the man,' was the idea. We dressed them in proper clothes and taught them the ABCs and 'Onward, Christian Soldiers' and all the rest.

"Well, that didn't sit too well with one redskin who called himself Strong Bull. He decided he'd 'Save the Indians, kill the missionaries.' And he did."

"But he got away from you," Snarf interrupted because he'd heard this story from DC.

"Yes, he got away. I don't begrudge him his escape, but the consequences suffered by me and mine, well, that I do begrudge. See, my son, his comportment and demeanor are not suited for rural life. He needs people and lots of them." Craney looked at the people walking to and fro through his town. He seemed to be looking at them from a great distance, as if they were small things in a tank that he was studying. As if he were a game warden and they were the game.

"'What man of you,'" Craney mused, "'if his son asks him for bread, will give him a stone? Or if he asks for a fish, will give him a serpent?'" He turned to Snarf. "I'm just trying to give my son something good. Would you begrudge me that?"

Snarf was too scared to answer.

Craney smiled, "I knew you wouldn't." He mussed Snarf's hair, then stood and looked out at his town. "You know what attracts people? Gold. A man will leave everything, his home, his family, his friends, even his faith for gold. The Ecstasy of Gold. All I've got to do is get the gold back, then people will come, and with them my son."

34

With a grunt, DC worked another heavy bag of gold off his shoulder and put it over Boss's back. The big horse blew and shook his head.

"He cannot carry so much," Redskin said and, indeed, Boss was greatly overloaded with bags of gold, for DC had refused to put any of them on Beautiful Feet. Only Mary Beth, the donkey, and Boss were permitted to carry DC's gold because their reins were all tied to DC's saddle.

The sheriff shot Redskin a glare as he untied his massive bedroll from the back of Boss's saddle. Once untied, he rolled it off his horse. Its leather covering slapped the ground. Boss sighed. Now he could tote the load.

DC waved his pistol at Redskin. Time to go.

Redskin led Beautiful Feet by the reins up the amphitheater steps. DC, with his pistol pointed at Redskin's back, followed with Boss, Mary Beth, and the donkey.

Redskin squeezed his way into the narrow channel of rock that led out out of the amphitheater and away from the cave.

"Hold it," DC said.

Redskin stopped.

"Come outta there," DC ordered.

"Why?"

"Why? Cause I said so."

Redskin backed Beautiful Feet out of the channel and saw the problem immediately; the horses couldn't fit through the channel with the bags of gold protruding from their sides.

"We'll carry it through," DC said. "Then reload the horses on the other end."

"We?" Redskin asked because so far, DC had not permitted him to touch the gold.

"Yes, *we*," DC said as if it was no big thing, when really it was. But they had to get the gold out, and fast. Something in him knew it had to be done fast. "Come here." DC put one of the heavy bags of gold over Redskin's shoulders then loaded one onto himself. They grunted and sweated their way through the channel. Once in the trees, they put the bags down. Redskin turned to go back for more, but DC didn't follow.

"Is something wrong?" Redskin asked.

DC was looking at the trees nervously. "Think anyone'll find it?"

"Before we get back with another load?" Redskin asked. "Not likely."

"Not likely," DC mused. "We'll bury it."

Neither of them moved.

"Which of us is to get the shovel?" Redskin asked.

"Stay here," DC snarled, "but don't touch it." He went back into the channel, walking backwards so he could keep his eyes and, more importantly, his pistol on Redskin.

Redskin watched the sheriff disappear into the rocky channel like a worm into its hole. Then he looked up at the few twinkling stars he could see through the trees. "Forgive me," he said. "Please, forgive me."

DC returned. He'd fetched a shovel from the donkey. He pushed it into Redskin's hands. "Bury it."

Redskin felt the thick wooden handle and the weight of the metal blade. One blow to the temple, and DC would be on the ground. Then he'd swing it over his head and bring it down like an ax. The blade was probably sharp enough to take the sheriff's head clean off; if it wasn't, well, the blow would break his neck.

DC cocked his pistol. "Bury it."

Redskin started digging.

"Bring the Indian or the gold to the top of the waterfall before midnight, or the boy hangs," the announcement broke through the silent forest.

Redskin straightened, tense, listening.

DC put a finger to his lips and pointed his pistol at Redskin's face.

"He's alive," Redskin whispered, the hope of a second chance filling him.

"Shut up," DC hissed.

"Bring the Indian or the gold to the top of the waterfall before midnight, or the boy hangs," the announcement came again, closer this time.

"DC-" Redskin stared to say, but DC clamped his hand over Redskin's mouth and dug his pistol into the Indian's chin. DC was close enough that he could see the veins pulsing in Redskin's neck, and Redskin could see the rage in the sheriff's eyes.

"Bring the Indian or the gold to the top of the waterfall before midnight, or the boy hangs." This time, the announcement was farther away.

But DC didn't move until the announcement came a fourth time from very far away. Then he said, "I'm gonna take my hand off your mouth, but you're not gonna scream or nothin."

Redskin nodded.

DC took his hand away. "Or the boy hangs," he muttered, looking toward the place the announcement had come from.

"It's a bluff," he decided, glancing at the gold. "Craney blew the kid to pieces and couldn't make nothin of the coyote, so he's tryin this."

"Do you really believe that?"

"Doesn't matter what I believe."

"What you believe is all that matters."

"Dig," DC ordered, backing up his command with his pistol.

Redskin lifted the shovel. One blow is all it would take- "DC, if you let that boy hang, your soul will be forfeit. You will burn."

DC smiled. "Burn. Who's gonna burn me?" he looked meaningfully at the shovel Redskin was strangling. "You?"

With visible effort, Redskin lowered the shovel.

DC stepped toward him. "Here's the thing: I ain't so sure I got a soul, but I'm real sure I got this gold. And I'm dead sure I'm gonna get off this mountain with every last bit of it. And you're gonna help me cause you can't hurt me or that soul of yours - which you're very certain you have - will be the one that burns. Am I right?"

He was.

"Good," DC said.

"Bring the Indian or the gold to the top of the waterfall before midnight, or the boy hangs," The announcement broke over them suddenly, very close.

"Get the gold!" DC hissed, thrusting one of the half-buried bags at Redskin, then shoving him back into the channel.

35

As Redskin crawled back through the throat of the coyote, he couldn't help but feel like he was being devoured. Not by the inanimate coyote, but by his own flesh. The man behind him, the man with the gun and the badge, was going to let Snarf hang so he could get his hands on some gold.

And he, Redskin, wasn't going to do a thing about it. What could he do? Kill? Yes, he could kill and easily, but that was exactly what his flesh wanted him to do. And Redskin knew that if he killed DC, he wouldn't be able to stop. He'd slaughter every man on this mountain. And Jewel too. Of that he was certain.

But he was going to save Snarf, whatever the cost. Of that he was even more certain.

He stepped out of the coyote's throat. The cave was all empty darkness ahead of him, except for the gold, which they'd piled in the saddle bags on the floor.

DC stepped out behind him. Redskin felt the sheriff's gun in his back. "Get outta the way," he ordered, but Redskin couldn't move. His body was frozen, his soul in turmoil. "Move!" DC barked.

Redskin's hand shot up into the darkness and found a hidden lever there. He pulled it. Air blasted him in the face. Something heavy and wooden boomed.

DC fired - the shot was like thunder and lightning in the dark cave - but Redskin was gone. DC had fired into empty air where a second ago there had been an Indian.

"Redskin?" he shouted, but he heard only an echo. "Redskin?" he yelled again, but still there was no answer.

He turned to the coyote and found the way blocked. Its throat clamped shut. He turned again to the cave. It was so quiet he could hear his heart pounding. "Redskin?" he shouted a third time, but still there was no answer. He lifted his torch high and advanced into the cave with his gun ready.

"Vengeance..." He heard Redskin mutter from somewhere in the darkness. "Vengeance is *mine*," Redskin bit the word "mine" off brutally. It was a moment before he finished the quotation, "saith the Lord..."

DC peered into the darkness. The echo made it impossible to tell where the Indian was.

Redskin was crouching in the darkness, his eyes squeezed shut and his body trembling - every muscle vibrating, like a weightlifter trying to hoist a ton. The muscles quivering under his red skin made it look like something in him really was alive, something very violent.

DC's torch roared as he waved it toward where he thought he'd heard a noise, but there was nothing there.

Redskin shook. He took off his shirt. It was soaked with some liquid that was dark and thick, darker and thicker than sweat. "Vengeance is mine," he whispered so softly only he could hear it. "Vengeance is mine, but... I am his instrument." Redskin opened his eyes. DC was a flame-gilded silhouette in the cave, not 10 footsteps away. And his back was to him.

DC licked his lips. The Indian could come at him from anywhere in this blackness.

Redskin's hand slid into one of the saddle bags and removed a gold bar.

DC saw him! His pistol flashed, blinding in the darkness. The bullet tore through the body. It slumped over, releasing a cloud of noxious gas, like a rotten egg. It wasn't Redskin; it was one of the corpses Billy'd made.

Redskin was behind DC, but the sheriff didn't know it. The Indian's scars gleamed in the torchlight. In fact, all of him shone. He glittered like a demon in hell. He glittered because he was covered in blood. His own blood that was oozing from every pore, drawn by the war of flesh and Spirit inside him. He raised the gold bar over DC's head, every muscle straining to bring it down with murderous force - Redskin twitched, a sudden hitch of movement. His hand holding the bar of gold over DC's skull faltered. "Forgive me," he whispered.

DC spun round, his pistol flashing and booming but hitting nothing because Redskin was crashing into him. DC grabbed Redskin, but he was slick with something. It felt hot and sticky.

The Indian wasn't fighting, DC realized somewhere in his mind, or he'd probably be dead already. He was trying to escape - he was trying to get to Craney! DC tightened his grip, but Redskin slid out like a fish and vanished in the darkness.

"You better not bring Craney here!" DC shouted. "I'll be ready, you hear me! I'll be ready!" But he heard only bare feet slapping into echoing distance. Eventually, all was silent again, except for the pounding of his heart.

DC rolled over, collected his gun from the place he'd dropped it, and went to the torch, which had been thrown in the fight. He took three bullets from his belt to reload. Once his hands were in the torchlight, however, he froze. They were covered in blood. He wiped them on his vest, but that only made it worse because there was blood all over his vest too. The Indian had been bleeding like a stuck pig. Why? He hadn't shot him. He'd shot enough men to know when he'd accomplished his aim, and he'd missed every time.

DC went to one of the corpses. Its clothing was bone dry. He wiped his hands on the cloth, being careful to scrub between his fingers and under the nails. In the fading torchlight, surrounded by bags of gold, with darkness closing in on him, DC cleaned his bloody hands with the clothes of a corpse.

36

Jewel's knitting needles clacked as she worked on a new pair of winter socks for Craney. Touchingly, she wore glasses while she knitted, to better see what her needles were doing.

Craney was not knitting. Nor was he holding the yarn, as was the custom of some helpful husbands. Nor was he reading. He was looking into the fire as he did every night, just watching it until it needed more fuel. Then he'd add wood until he was sure the fire would still be going when he woke. He did this because once, he'd thought that the fire had somehow gotten inside him. A draft of air had come swooping, like a bat, down the chimney. The fire had leapt at him, and he'd thought for sure he was burning. He'd fallen to the floor, screaming and thrashing until his mind went dark. When he woke, there were only ashes in the fireplace. The clock had said only a few minutes had passed, but he'd felt the ashes. They were dead cold. Since then, he always made sure the fire had enough fuel to last the night, and cold ashes unnerved him.

He stood and added another log. He watched the fire lap at it. He checked the clock: seven minutes to midnight. He opened the glass window covering the clockface. Jewel saw what he was doing and smiled at him. Craney advanced the clock to midnight.

The clock chimed. Snarf came awake in a flash, in time to hear the last portentous chimes.

"Let's take a walk," Craney said.

The night was cool. Snarf could just see the tiniest wisps of breath coming from the mouths of the soldiers who were hastily assembling - after all, things were starting a few minutes ahead of schedule. The women and children leaned out of the open windows and doorways of their homes to watch the procession.

Flint had put up torches around the perimeter of the outcropping. Their blazing light outlined the dangling noose and cast a hellish glow on the water as it went streaming eternally past.

Snarf dug his heels into the ground.

"C'mon, son," Craney said, grabbing Snarf's arm and dragging him toward the noose.

"Stop calling me that," Snarf said through clenched teeth as he tried to tear himself away. But Craney's grip was iron. They moved inexorably toward the noose, like Abraham and Isaac toward the pyre.

"What would you like me to call you?"

"DC!" Snarf screamed, hoping the sheriff, wherever he was, would hear him.

"Ok. DC it is then."

They were on the outcropping now. Snarf could hear the mist from the waterfall hissing in the torches. Flint slipped the noose over his head.

"Any last words, DC?" Craney asked Snarf.

"Please," Snarf begged, "please, just a few more minutes. DC'll come. You said he'd come."

"I did," Craney said. "But it looks like I was wrong, and we like our trains to run on time." He grabbed Snarf's collar and pushed him toward the edge of the outcropping.

Snarf clamped both his hands around Craney's wrist. One of his feet slipped on the wet rock and dangled in empty space. He scrambled for purchase and managed to get both toes back on the rock. He hung suspended with a noose around his neck, his hands clamped around Craney's wrist, his toes on the rock, and the sound of the waterfall roaring in his ears.

"Please!" he begged.

"Let go."

"Please!"

"There was one guy wouldn't let go until we put a torch to him. Candelabra we called him."

"Please!"

"Let. Go."

"Stop!" someone shouted.

Craney and everyone else turned toward the speaker.

It was Redskin.

He stood shirtless in the misty torchlight, covered from head to toe in blood. "Here am I," he announced.

"You bring the gold?" Craney asked.

"I can take you to it."

Craney looked Redskin up and down as he considered. The Indian seemed to be covered in blood. "I believe you can," he announced, hauling Snarf back onto the outcropping.

Snarf's knees buckled, and he collapsed. Panting, on his hands and knees, he felt someone take the noose off him. He looked up into Redskin's face. "DC?" he asked.

"With the gold," Redskin answered gently.

"What happened? To you, I mean."

Redskin smiled, "I survived the coyote and earned my name."

"You killed your flesh?" Snarf asked.

"I dealt it a blow."

"You said your partner's with the gold," Craney interrupted. "If he runs off with it, I'll kill you both."

"He won't," Redskin said. He helped Snarf to his feet and said to him, "You should stay here."

"No way!"

"DC is... you may not like what you see."

"Is he hurt?" Snarf asked, frightened at the prospect.

"No."

"I'm coming with you." Snarf insisted, wondering what could have possibly happened to the sheriff.

37

Craney's impressed whistle echoed through the great underground Indian amphitheater. "Under my nose the whole time," he said as his men filed in around him.

"Your gold is inside the coyote," Redskin said, pointing to the stage. "As is DC. I fear he will not turn it over without a fight."

"I can be persuasive," Craney replied. "Can you open it?"

"I can, but he may fire at us."

Snarf climbed onto the stage. Mary Beth, Beautiful Feet, Boss, and the donkey stood by the coyote. They looked relieved to see him. He gave Mary Beth a hug. Jewel watched jealously.

"Clear away," Craney hollered at his men. Flint cleared them away from the mouth of the coyote, so any shots from inside would just go into the stone bleachers.

Redskin went to the great snarling head and pulled one of the ears. There was a thunk as a piece of wood somewhere swung aside. But otherwise, all was silent inside the coyote.

Craney lit a cigarette. Then he shouted from his place at the coyote's cheek, "DC!"

Gunshots blasted out of the coyote's mouth and ricocheted off the stone bleachers. Everyone ducked and covered.

"Come on," Craney yelled. "You think I'm stupid enough to stand in front of this thing?"

"Don't come in here!"

"I will eventually. The only question is if you'll be alive when I do."

"Redskin got outta here somehow."

"He did, but you've been in there a while now, and you haven't spent a second looking for the way out. Am I right?"

DC made no answer.

"It's called the Ecstasy of Gold," Craney explained. "It comes on men when they find a big haul. I've seen it before. So, you want me to take care of this quick, or you want me to wait until you starve?"

"Do it quick!"

"You got it," Craney said, straightening and taking a stick of dynamite from his belt. He lifted the fuse to his cigarette.

"Wait," Snarf interrupted. "Can I go in there? And talk to him? Maybe he'll come out."

"Maybe," Craney said, doubting it. He looked at Jewel.

"I think he's old enough to go by himself, if he wants to," she said.

"The kid wants to go in there," Craney shouted into the coyote's mouth. "What do you think?"

A few heartbeats passed. "Send him in," came DC's answer.

Snarf made to climb into the coyote's mouth, but Redskin grabbed his arm. "No, Snarf, he's a Fleshwalker."

"So am I," Snarf said, "and I want him alive."

Redskin saw in the boy's eyes that he loved DC more than anything. So he let him go.

"Hey, son," Craney said, "you might need this." He was holding out Snarf's gunbelt.

Snarf took it from him and strapped it on.

Redskin tore his eyes away from the boy who was about to be devoured by the coyote and looked at the invisible person to his right.

Snarf, staring into the gaping maw of the coyote, took a deep breath. Then he climbed in.

38

The Spartans, those ancient warriors who saved the West by dying to the last man in a tiny gorge called The Hot Gates, made a science of fear. They discovered that different types of fear lived in different places of the body. The worst kind of fear, the kind of fear that could unman even the strongest men, lived in the throat, they believed. That is why the Spartans always sang on their way into battle, to get out their fear and to give it to their enemies.

In Snarf's time, Stonewall Jackson, the great general of the Confederacy, also knew fear lived in the throat. That is why he commanded his men, "When you charge, yell like furies!" They did, and the spine-tingling Rebel Yell was born and it almost shattered the Union. Perhaps it was something similar that happened to the walls of Jericho.

Unfortunately, Snarf knew none of this, so as he crawled down the coyote's throat, with his own throat tightening, he did not sing. He did not speak. He barely breathed. He did, however, wretch in the noxious air. Then he tumbled out of the throat and into the darkness of the cave.

He climbed to his feet, brushing himself off and shivering

like a newborn. Then he saw DC. The sheriff, inspired perhaps by the original wall of gold, had constructed himself a foxhole of gold. He was inside it, aiming his pistol at Snarf through the little window.

Snarf put up his hands.

"Get in here," DC urged, waving with his pistol.

Snarf scurried around and climbed in beside the sheriff, who never took his eyes off the coyote's throat, lest someone try and sneak in after Snarf.

"Glad to see you, deputy," he said, making Snarf beam, but then he went on, "with the two of us we got a chance. Yer gun's a little wild, but one blast down that tunnel will make em think twice. All we gotta do is find the way outta here that Indian took."

"DC, I'm not here to help you get the gold," Snarf confessed.

"Not here to help. What are you here for?"

"To save you."

DC scoffed. "Save me. How're you gonna do that?"

"Well, I was thinking I'd just tell you that if you didn't come out and let Craney have the gold, he'd dynamite you."

"And then you thought I'd come out?"

Snarf nodded.

DC laughed. "That's a mighty simple plan you had there, deputy. I got a simpler one: Craney shows his face in that tunnel to toss in a stick of dynamite or whatever, and I shoot him. Then *I* keep the gold."

Snarf didn't know what to say. He hadn't expected DC to resist. The impossibility of the situation was so obvious.

"How's it goin in there?" Craney hollered down the tunnel.

"Fine," DC hollered back. "Thanks for sendin me another gun."

"My pleasure. You've got one minute to get out or I'll blast you both."

"We ain't comin out!"

Snarf couldn't believe it. "DC," he said, "DC, he means it."

"So do I."

"He'll blow you up."

"Me? You're in here too, deputy, or were you thinkin of runnin out?"

"Thirty seconds," Craney announced.

"I- I don't know."

"Don't know? Well, you better make up your mind."

Snarf swallowed and looked toward the coyote's throat.

"Fifteen seconds."

"I think..." Snarf trailed off, unable to make up his mind.

"Ten seconds."

"I..."

"Five seconds."

"I'll stay with you!" Snarf declared, hunkering down beside the sheriff.

DC mussed his hair and slapped him on the back. "That's my boy," he said.

Snarf drew Pap's Pistol and pointed it through the gilded window at the coyote's throat. They lay pressed together, the boy and the sheriff, in a foxhole made of gold in the belly of a coyote, with their guns drawn and their hearts ready to explode.

But nothing happened.

No hand tossed a stick of hissing dynamite down the coyote's throat. No blast of fire consumed them, tearing them to pieces.

Eventually, Craney spoke, his voice hard and cold, "You didn't tell me who your friend was."

Snarf and DC looked at each other. They had no idea what Craney was talking about.

"Turns out *Redskin*," he said the name sarcastically, "and I go way back. Only when I knew him, he went by Strong Bull."

Snarf's insides went suddenly cold. "Strong Bull," he whispered, "but that's the Indian who Craney-"

DC understood. "What's your quarrel with him got to do with us?"

"Not a thing. Except that if you don't come out, I'll kill him. Then I'll bast you. Awful thing to die with on your conscience. But, if you come out now, I'll let him live. I get the gold, and ya'll go home. One big, happy family."

"Happy family," DC muttered. "Kill him," he declared. "He means nothin to me."

Snarf couldn't believe it.

"What's the boy have to say about it?" Craney asked.

"He's with me," DC declared.

Then the sheriff felt Snarf move. He turned slowly toward the sound and found himself staring down six enormous barrels. Snarf was behind Pap's Pistol, with hot tears running down his cheeks. His lip was quivering, and that made him even angrier. "I'm not with you," Snarf said, meaning it in every possible way.

DC snorted. "You gonna shoot me?"

"I will if you don't walk outta here."

"Will that thing even fire?"

The moment the question left DC's lips, Snarf fired past his ear. Only a single round went off. It ricocheted through the cave, ending in an echoing silence somewhere in the depths of the earth.

"We cleaned it, remember," Snarf said.

"I remember." He let Snarf take his pistol.

"Who's dead?" Craney hollered.

"Nobody," Snarf replied, training both guns on DC. "We're comin out." He motioned for DC to get up.

The sheriff climbed out of the golden foxhole and walked toward the coyote's throat with Snarf behind him. He bent and looked out the coyote's throat. He could see only a narrow oval of the amphitheater, Flint in the center with the rest of Craney's men arrayed, guns drawn, around him. Craney himself stood to the side with his gun digging into Redskin's side. Jewel was with him.

"You know," DC said, "I don't think you've got the guts." He spun, fist raised and aimed at Snarf's head like a battering ram.

Snarf flinched back. Something bucked in his right hand. His knuckles felt heat. The little hairs on them spun into coils and blackened. A flash blinded him. He thought for sure it was the impact of DC's fist on his face, but it couldn't have been because DC was gone.

He blinked, trying to clear the stars from his vision. The sharp smell of gunpowder burned in his nose. In the darkness of the cave, Pap's Pistol glowed red with hellfire and blood.

Someone coughed. It was an unhealthy, wet cough.

DC lay on the ground, his chest a bloody ruin. Snarf dropped both guns and ran to his hero. DC's chest heaved in a ragged breath. "You shot me," he said, not quite believing the kid had had the guts.

Snarf was so shocked by what he'd done, he could hardly think. "I'm sorry," he said. The words sounded hopelessly little. But what were you supposed to say when you'd blown a man open? He didn't have a clue.

DC shook his head, "Don't be." With trembling hands, he took off his sheriff's badge and gave it to Snarf. It was slick with his blood. "You earned it, deputy."

"But you're sheriff," Snarf insisted, trying to give it back, hoping that would somehow take back what he'd done.

DC shook his head, "Sheriff? Not anymore."

Snarf sobbed.

"It's ok. You did the right thing. Hey," DC said, demanding Snarf's attention, "you're one tough barve."

Snarf smiled a smile wet with tears. He wiped the blood off

the badge and felt the letters that made up the word 'SHER-IFF'. They'd been pressed into the metal, stamped there by heat and fire. Once a man was branded with a silver star, only death could take it off.

"Gimme," DC whispered, "gimme some gold."

Snarf stuffed the badge into his pocket and went to the golden foxhole. He grabbed a bar and carried it with both hands to DC. He set it down, and DC rested his hand on it. "It's cold," he said. "I always hated bein cold."

Those were DC's last words.

39

Snarf looked down at the body of the first man he'd ever killed on purpose. Had he killed DC on purpose? Had he fired at Flint, back in The Six, on purpose? Or had something, something crazy and wild, grabbed hold of him both times and made him do it? After all, he hadn't been able to shoot the outlaw in Ithaca or the outlaw in the crater...

A man could pull a trigger in a second, but what happened after went on forever.

DC had spun, and he'd felt Pap's Pistol buck.

It was instinct.

No, that wasn't it. Not exactly. Instincts are deep things, too deep to be invented in a flash of gunpowder.

Snarf realized then that long ago, he'd made a decision. At some point, he didn't know when, he'd decided, deep down, that he wanted to be more like Redskin than DC. And that decision, a decision he didn't even known he'd made, had made him kill the sheriff. He felt like a traitor.

He left the guns where he'd dropped them and crawled out of the coyote's mouth. He stood before Craney and his army.

He couldn't look at any of them. He kept his eyes on the bloody red stage. "DC's dead," he said quietly.

Craney gave Flint a nod. Flint drew his gun, in case it was a setup, and went into the coyote. A moment later he shouted out, "He's dead, an all the gold's here."

Craney's men poured around Snarf and into the coyote's mouth. Craney knelt on his bad knees so he could look Snarf in the eye, but Snarf kept his eyes on the floor. Craney put his hands gently on Snarf's shoulders, commanding his attention. "Thank you," Craney said. There was real gratitude in his eyes. "If you don't have anywhere to go... I could use someone like you."

Snarf didn't know what to say to the unexpected offer.

With a whoop, one of the soldiers emerged from the coyote's mouth. He slapped one of the gold bars into Craney's hand. Craney held it for a moment, feeling its weight - the weight of a promise made to a son long ago. He held it out to Snarf, "I pay well."

Snarf took the bar. It was very heavy and there was something about the gold that seemed to call to him... then he saw that the gold was marred by a bloody handprint. He didn't know it, but it was Redskin's handprint. This was the very bar of gold Redskin had raised to bash in DC's skull. He gave it back to Craney. "You promised me Redskin."

"And you believed me?" Craney asked. When he saw that Snarf had, he tipped his head back and laughed. It echoed through the amphitheater. Jewel, with her derringer pressed to Redskin's side, laughed too. Craney rose unsteadily on his bad knees. He mussed Snarf's hair. "You're too gullible, son."

It had all been for nothing. He'd killed DC for nothing. Unk had died for nothing. He'd come all this way for nothing. He'd collected Wanted posters and dreamed of being sheriff for nothing. Every single moment of his life had been wasted.

He'd failed at everything. He wished he were swinging over the waterfall.

Craney pointed a thumb at the horses his men were loading up with gold. "Which one of these is yours?"

Snarf just stood there, dead to the world. So Mary Beth took the initiative and stepped forward.

"Leave her for the kid," Craney ordered.

"With the gold?" Flint asked.

"Yeah, with the gold," Craney spat, mocking Flint's toothless voice.

"But how will we get–"

"You'll carry it!" Craney shouted. "I thought it was teeth you didn't have, not brains."

Flint and the others scrambled to unload Mary Beth. Once she was free, she went to Snarf, but he didn't move. She made her reins brush his hand. Reflexively, he gripped them. Mary Beth led him toward Redskin. She gave Jewel a look and the woman stepped back.

Snarf, his eyes on the floor, knew he was standing in front of Redskin. He took a shuddering breath. "I killed him," he confessed.

"I know," Redskin said, his voice soft.

"I think I killed him to save you."

"I know."

"But– but it didn't work." Snarf's lips trembled as he fought back tears.

"I know," Redskin repeated, his heart breaking for the boy.

Craney came and grabbed Redskin's arm. "See you around, son," he said as he dragged Redskin away. Snarf never did look up at Redskin. He couldn't. Jewel put her arm through Craney's as they walked up the amphitheater steps with their prisoner.

Flint put something big and heavy on Mary Beth. "You can keep this," he said. It was DC's body. Flint shoved Pap's Pistol into the back of DC's belt. "Maybe put it on yer wall," he laughed an ugly, hateful laugh and followed Craney and the soldiers out of the amphitheater.

Soon Snarf, Mary Beth, and DC's corpse were alone in the dark, with the coyote snarling behind them. Mary Beth started up the steps, pulling Snarf along behind her. She led him out of the dark cave, through the narrow channel of rock, and into the pale light of dawn.

40

Mary Beth led Snarf to the Indian graveyard. He put Pap's Pistol back on his belt, and he put DC in one of the graves then pushed the dirt over him. He took off his hat and closed his eyes. He listened to the distant roar of the waterfall, the nearby patter of the river, and the occasional clink of Mary Beth's harness as she stood beside him. He felt the air warming as the sun rose.

Finally, he snarfed and admitted to the buried body of his hero, "I wanted to be just like you. You were strong and brave and- and you were good. I thought." He hung his head. "I'd hoped..." His jaw worked as he tried to figure out what it was that he'd hoped, "I'd hoped you would be like my dad after Unk..." he trailed off. "But seems like I'm gonna be ridin by myself a while yet." Mary Beth nuzzled him. He buried his face in her mane. Eventually, he looked down at the grave again. "G'bye," he said.

Then he put on his hat, wiped his eyes, and turned to Mary Beth, but he froze. There was a man standing on the other side of DC's grave. Snarf had not heard him approach. He looked at the man, but as he looked at him, he could not see him.

Looking at the man was like looking at the sun. You can see it, you know it's there, but you can't actually look at it.

And the heat!

The heat radiating from the man drove Snarf to his knees. It penetrated his clothes, his skin, his bones, his brain, his very being. The heat bore into Snarf and bore down on him. He lay on his face and spread his arms wide. "You're Him," he said.

"I am," the man answered.

The heat trebled. Snarf thought he was going to come apart. He gasped at the pain. Every inch of him felt stinging heat, like cold, numb hands plunged into hot water. "I want to be a Spiritwalker!" he cried desperately.

In a flash, the heat transformed. It still penetrated every particle of him, but it no longer bore down on him, and he no longer felt like he was going to come apart, and he no longer felt its sting. Instead, he felt light, whole, and he felt like he wanted to-

"Rise," the Son of the Great Father said. "Do not be afraid."

Snarf rose and found he could look at the Son of the Great Father now, although there was something about his sight that told him he was still seeing without seeing, like he was looking at a veil or curtain that had caught an image of that which is beyond sight.

The Son of the Great Father was dressed like a general in Union blue. His brown boots were well worn. His beard was black and thick, although it was close cut. His skin was brown and, Snarf thought, comforting, like earth. But his forehead was laced with awful scars like the ones on Redskin's torso. He held his hat at his side. He wore no gun, but a saber glittered at his hip. And instead of medals on his breast, there was a star of the purest and brightest silver Snarf had ever seen.

And his eyes. The steady, comforting fire in them burned into Snarf with the unshakable light of an ocean of suns. Snarf wanted nothing more in that moment than for the moment itself to go on forever and ever without end. But he felt himself compelled to say, "I want to be a Spiritwalker. What must I do?"

The Son of the Great Father looked at something high up behind Snarf. He turned to follow the gaze and saw the water-fall, gilded by the rising sun, and the gallows, still in shadow, on the outcropping. Craney must be nearly there. With Redskin.

"His hour has not yet come," the Son of the Great Father said.

"But I'll die," Snarf said.

"You will be born again, I promise."

Snarf looked back at the outcropping. It was high, and it was far, and Craney had a head start. Pap's Pistol hung heavy on his belt. The idea of using it again made him sick. Then he felt something on his belt. Redskin's knife. *That* he could use.

Snarf turned to the Son of the Great Father, but he was gone. He'd left as silently as he came. The only traces of his presence were the prints his boots made in the mud and the fire of his promise now glowing in Snarf's eyes.

Snarf started to snarf but caught himself. He wasn't nervous or even afraid. He put his arm down. "Come on, Mary Beth," he said, his voice trembling but finding its determination. "Let's go." He climbed onto her back, put his heels to her flank, and she shot up the mountain.

Snarf's gallop up the mountain with Mary Beth was the wildest of his life. Riding bareback, he clung to the reins, but he needn't have been afraid. She was not going to let him fall. She'd been made for this. She ran faster up the mountain that morning than she'd run on the flat plain all those days ago. She ran faster that golden morning than she would ever run in all the rest of her days; a power lent her strength and speed beyond that of all mortal horses.

But not beyond that of all immortal horses.

Snarf saw a flash of white in the corner of his eye. There was a white stallion galloping beside them, and the Son of the Great Father was on his back! He extended his saber like a general leading a charge, and Snarf saw that there was some wound, like a bullet hole, long healed, on his wrist. The white horse threw back its head and neighed. Snarf's heart leapt with a joy known only to the dolphins that leap out of blue waters into kaleidoscopes of sunshine. Mary Beth neighed and galloped after them, but the white horse was too fast. They lost sight of him and his rider, but their determination did not flag, and their hearts did not sink. They both knew that the Son of the Great Father and his white horse were charging ahead of them. There was nothing to fear. Not even Craney. Not even death. The Son of the Great Father had promised.

41

Mary Beth slowed to a stop on the outskirts of Craney's town. Snarf dismounted and peered through the trees. The whole town was celebrating like it was Independence Day. A brass band marched down the main street, leading the men with the gold. Behind them came Redskin, his hands tied behind his back, with Craney and Jewel on either side. The half-naked children danced in the dirt around them. The procession was heading for the bank.

"We have to find Beautiful Feet," Snarf whispered to Mary Beth.

She understood and led him to the right. He followed her until he saw the backside of the stable. Beautiful Feet, Boss, and the donkey were all there. Snarf slipped across the bit of empty ground and into the stable.

Beautiful Feet blew when she saw him.

"Shhhh!" Snarf said with a finger to his lips. He untied all of them. They saw Mary Beth on the border of the forest and hurried to her. Snarf turned to follow them, but something caught his eye. A stack of crates. The one on top had straw coming out of it.

Mary Beth made a sound. Snarf looked at her. She wanted him to come to her, but he wanted to know what was in those crates. He put up a finger to tell her he'd be right there.

He lifted away a handful of straw and saw a neat row of red cylinders. "Kolowissi," he breathed. There was enough dynamite in the stable to blow away the whole side of the mountain, to wipe out Craney and his entire town!

Snarf found a bag stuffed behind the crates. He opened it. Fuse cord. He pulled a few arm lengths of the stuff out, enough to give him and the horses a head start after they'd rescued Redskin, and cut it with his knife.

Then the music stopped.

Snarf peeped out of the stable. The whole town stood in front of the bank. Craney was making a speech with Jewel at his side while the men carried the gold into the bank one bar at a time.

Flint stood at the back of the crowd with his pistol pressed to Redskin's side. A little girl left the crowd - speeches didn't interest her - and walked up to Redskin in that forward way children have when they see something strange. Redskin looked down at her, and she looked up at him. She said something to him, but Snarf couldn't hear because he was too far away. Redskin put out his bound hands for her to touch. She extended a single delicate white finger and poked the back of his red hand. She drew her finger back fast and clutched it to her chest, as if she'd touched a stove, but Redskin hadn't moved. She smiled up at him. He smiled at her. Then her mother saw her near the savage Indian and dragged her away.

Snarf looked back at the crates of dynamite. He couldn't blow up the whole town. He lifted a single red stick. How was *he* supposed to save Redskin anyway?

The band started again. They were coming back, this time with Redskin at the head and Craney and Jewel on either side. They were leading him to the gallows!

Snarf grabbed the stick of dynamite and ran out of the stable. He hunkered down behind it as the people paraded past. He checked around the corner. The bank was deserted.

Mary Beth watched him intently. "Go," he mouthed at her. She nodded and led the other horses and the donkey into the woods.

Snarf looked back at the bank. It was completely abandoned. He looked toward the gallows. Every back was turned. It was now or never.

42

Flint thought he saw something.

It was probably a trick of the light, a bit of sunshine playing off a window, but it gnawed at him. He'd seen it streak across the road toward the bank. If it had been any other building, he wouldn't have made the effort, but the bank was important.

He ducked out of the crowd. Craney was doing this hanging himself anyway; he wouldn't be missed, and God knew he'd seen enough hangings. Craney never lost his interest in them, but Flint was bored stiff of hangings. He hadn't even bothered to hang his clothes in years; that's how tired he was of hangings.

His boots creaked down the street toward the bank.

He stood at the door, studying it. It was open. Just a crack, but it *was* open. He sucked his tooth.

He took his bandana out of his pocket and tied it over his mutilated face. People thought he wore the bandana cause he was vain. He wasn't. He'd lost his vanity a long, long time ago. No, he wore the bandana cause one time, when he'd shot a man close, a drop of the man's blood had gotten in his mouth. He hadn't liked that.

He pushed the door with his pistol. It swung open freely without squeaking. The hinges were new.

The bank was as empty as it'd been when they'd left it.

Flint's boots thumped across the floor toward the teller line. A little half-door separated the teller line from the bank floor. Flint opened it without stepping through. Nothing happened. He sank onto his hams and leaned around the corner with his gun ready. But there was no one under the teller line.

He stood up.

He cocked an ear, listening. The waterfall roared... Craney made his speech... There was something more... Some other sound...

Flint cocked his pistol and stalked toward the open vault door. All the big city banks left their vault doors open during the day: too much aggravation to open and close it every time a customer wanted to make a withdrawal. And it announced to everybody that you weren't afraid of nothin. Flint could respect that. So could Craney; that's why he insisted the vault door always be left open.

Flint put his back to the wall beside the open vault. Sure enough, the noise was coming from inside.

He swung into the vault, pistol leveled and finger on the trigger. But it was just a vault filled with gold.

And a stick of dynamite with a spark hissing its way through the last inch of fuse.

Flint was afraid.

43

Craney and Jewel walked Redskin to the noose. Craney had his gold bar, the one Redskin had almost killed DC with, in his hand. The entire town was watching. The water, shining golden in the sunlight, thundered past. The mist made the dried blood covering Redskin wet again. It glistened and ran down his arms and chest in red streaks. He looked like he'd been skinned alive.

"When we hung Murton, what'd we call him?" Craney asked Jewel.

"Haunted," Jewel answered, "Haunted Murton."

"That's right. Haunted Murton we called him. He was an arsonist. Burnt up a whole church with the congregation inside it just for fun. Anyway, when we hung him, he started screaming - best he could with the rope tight round his neck - that he could hear them singing. Took us a minute to figure out he meant he could hear the people he'd burned. Now, I think a lot about Haunted Murton because, where did the voices come from?"

Redskin said nothing.

Craney studied the gold bar in his hand. The mist had wetted the blood on it. He wiped it off with his sleeve. "You know where I think they came from? I think they came from the water. Which makes me wonder - are you gonna hear them? Are you gonna hear the cries of the missionaries you killed when you burned their schools? Are you gonna hear the screams of the teachers as you... you know."

Redskin just looked at him, unaffected by the taunting and unafraid of Craney. Craney put the noose around Redskin's neck. Jewel cinched it tight, like a tie.

Craney leaned in to Redskin's ear and whispered, "If you do hear them, you give a little shout, because I'd like to know."

"I have been washed of their blood," Redskin said.

Craney ran his hand up Redskin's back and held it out so he could see. It was covered with blood. "Looks like you need another bath." With his blood-covered hand, Craney pushed Redskin off the outcropping.

Redskin didn't cry out or grab for the rope or struggle in any way. He swung silently and gently, like the pendulum of a great clock. For a moment, Craney, Jewel, and the whole town were transfixed by the beauty of the red Indian soaring through the golden mist. He swung into the white cataract of falling water, creating a great billow of mist, like a cloud. A rainbow appeared in the cloud.

Craney roared, "He's like an angel!"

The town erupted with cheers and laughter. Some flapped their arms in mockery of flight. Others laced their fingers together, put them to their cheeks, and blinked innocently, like cherubs.

Redskin kept his eyes lightly shut, waiting patiently for his forever life to begin while the noose tightened around his neck.

Jewel slipped her hand into Craney's. He smiled at her. She smiled back and said, "He was an evil man. You did good."

"Matthew Craney!" The cry came loud and clear over the roaring water.

They all turned.

Redskin opened his eyes. Through the spots that were forming in his vision, he saw Snarf standing alone in the middle of the street. He stood like DC had on the rim of the depression, tall and straight and bold with the sheriff's badge glittering on his chest.

"What?" Craney shouted back, exasperated and a little amused by the boy's tenacity.

Snarf pointed his knife at Redskin, who was still swinging. "Let him go."

"No," Craney replied, wondering where the kid had gotten the gumption. Then the earth shook under him. And the wheels of time slowed.

Behind the boy, his bank, newly packed with gold, swelled. As it swelled, red fire oozed between the whitewashed siding, blackening the new wood and devouring the gold. The townspeople shied away from the blast, making way left and right for Snarf, who was charging through them. Craney and Jewel watched him pass, too stunned to do anything. Then Snarf leapt off the outcropping and into empty space.

The wheels of time caught and flew on again.

Snarf's arms and legs pinwheeled. He collided with the rope. He wrapped himself around it and slid down, clear down until he was sitting on Redskin's head. He put his knife to the rope and sawed.

Craney saw the sunlight flash off the blade. Rage filled him like the shadow from the fireplace had that dark night long ago when he'd decided to send his son away instead of kill him like he should have.

He drew.

Snarf looked right at him.

Their eyes locked.

Then the knife went through the rope, and Snarf and Redskin vanished into the waterfall.

44

The river flowed lightly past the Indian graveyard. Mary Beth, Beautiful Feet, Boss, and the donkey came out of the forest and looked around, but they were alone. While they waited, they sniffed and nudged each other to keep their spirits up. A light fog rose from the river as the dawning sun warmed its surface.

Their ears pricked up. Someone was wading toward them. A dark figure appeared in the fog. It was carrying something. They watched intently. Beautiful Feet stamped.

Redskin materialized out of the fog.

He was carrying Snarf.

The boy was limp.

Redskin waded onto shore and dropped to his knees in front of the horses, whose eyes were wide with watching. He put his hand to Snarf's chest, to feel the life pounding in him, but he felt nothing.

Mary Beth sniffed Snarf's wet hair. She nuzzled his face with her soft nose, but the boy didn't move. She buried her face in Beautiful Feet's mane.

Redskin's eyes were distant, looking at nothing, but they

caught on something. Or someone. His eyes traveled up, as if moving up a person's legs. Finally, they stopped at about the level of a man's face.

Mary Beth pulled her head out of Beautiful Feet's mane and looked at the same invisible person Redskin was looking at.

"Did you choose him?" Redskin asked. A moment later, the Indian nodded. "Thank you," he said, a smile fighting its way through his tears. He squeezed Snarf's body, tight, and took a deep shuddering breath through his ruined throat. He whimpered as he held Snarf and rocked him, weeping hot tears.

Mary Beth watched, miserable because she had not been given the stuff she needed to be able cry, although she wanted to cry very, very badly.

Eventually, Redskin stood. He carried Snarf's body to the empty grave beside DC's and put the boy in it. He fit in the grave with room to spare. He crossed Snarf's hands over his chest and smoothed his shirt so the badge was straight. Finally, he climbed out of the grave. He took up a handful of dirt. "The Great Father gave, and the Great Father hath taken away; blessed be the Great Father." He tossed his handful of dirt onto Snarf's chest.

Snarf coughed! He coughed, and he tried to sit up. But he hadn't the strength, so he rolled over. Water gushed out of him. He'd drunk half the river! He felt someone's hands lifting him, and he heard someone laughing. A horse somewhere was neighing. None of it made any sense after such a long time in the dark.

He blinked, and Redskin's face swam into view. Mary Beth was there too. And Beautiful Feet, and Boss, and even Billy's donkey, but he kept on looking, looking around for someone he expected to see, but did not. "I saw him. Where-"

"He's here," Redskin soothed.

"Where?" Snarf was desperate.

"Just there."

Snarf looked at the place and saw nothing. "I don't see him."

"He's there."

"I can't see him. Redskin, why can't I see him?"

"Shhhhh," Redskin patted him. "Even I do not see him always."

"I wanna see him always. I want to follow him. I want to be a Spiritwalker like you."

Redskin regarded Snarf. The boy meant it. "It will cost you everything."

"Everything?" Snarf looked at the boot prints left by the Son of the Great Father and remembered the heat. "I don't reckon he's the kind to horse trade. I'll pay."

"Yes," Redskin said, feeling the weight of the boy's words even if the boy himself was too young to feel it, "yes, I believe you will. And I'll help," he said as he helped Snarf to his feet.

Snarf patted Mary Beth, and she put her head on his shoulder while Beautiful Feet nuzzled his hand. He smiled at them both. It felt wonderful to be alive. Then he saw the outcropping, smoking high up on the mountainside.

"Kolowissi?" Redskin asked.

"Kolowissi," Snarf said, wondering what was going on up there, wondering if he'd ever see Craney again.

Redskin mounted Beautiful Feet. Snarf climbed onto Mary Beth's bare back.

"You ride like an Indian," Redskin said.

"I ride like a Spiritwalker," Snarf replied.

Redskin laughed.

They rode off together into the rising sun, leaving behind two graves: one filled with a corpse, the other empty, as if the body in it had been resurrected.

SNARF'S ADVENTURES
CONTINUE...

Spiritwalkers don't ride alone! The best way for you to continue your adventure with Snarf and Redskin is to tell a friend about this book or even let them borrow it!

While you're sharing this book with a friend, I'm working hard on book 2! If you sign up for my newsletter today, you'll be the first to know when it's ready, and you'll be the first to know Snarf's real name... Also, if you sign up now, I'll send you a prequel chapter - before Redskin was Redskin, he was Strong Bull, a brutal Indian brave; before Craney was Craney, he was Captain Craney, commander of the troops of Ft. Bowie; see their final, fiery confrontation by signing up for my newsletter:
lmhelm.com/spiritwalkernewsletter

Reviews are more encouraging than you know, so please leave a review on social media or wherever you purchased this book. Even if it's only a line or two, it will help others find this book and it will be a great encouragement to me.

You can download FREE digital wallpapers at store.lmhelm.com

I'd love to hear from you! Email me via the contact form on my website (lmhelm.com) and I'll respond as soon as I can.